Nose Dive

NOSE DIVE

by

Karin Gustafson

Illustrated by Jonathan Segal

BACKSTROKE BOOKS

Other books by Karin Gustafson

1 Mississippi

Going on Somewhere

ISBN: 0981992331

ISBN-13: 9780981992334

For Meredith, Christina, Rhona.

NOSE DIVE

I.

(The hills are alive...with the sound of music.)

Maybe. But first period assembly was comatose with the boredom of teenagers. Even people's yawns stretched out in slow-mo.

(A song they have sung...for a thousand years.)

Then Brad Pierson sauntered to the podium. A lot of yawns filled instantly with drool.

"Yo Brad," some girl wailed.

Brad smiled. It was a sheepish, glinty smile, the kind that commercials flash above surfboards.

I looked back down to my Bio notes, trying to cram for my next period test. Brad was in my Pre-Cal class but that was about the only thing we had in common: he was captain of the tennis team and hung out with the cool popular kids while I sang in the school chorus and hung out with Deanna, my one true friend since age five. Deanna was plenty cool in her way, but I wasn't. For example, the title song of *The Sound of Music* was just then spinning around my head.

(*The hills fill my heart with the sound of music.*)

I really love *The Sound of Music*—actually, I love the sound of almost any music—but I wouldn't mind if it stayed clear of my brain once in a while.

Brad, after gently adjusting the microphone, gave a cute little waist-level wave.

'*ATP stands for*—' I scribbled in my notebook.

"With the help of Principal Eggars—" Brad said.

(*My heart wants to sing every song....*)

"—I'm arranging for the spring musical to be part of a new TV reality show."

The auditorium inhaled one huge "omg." Even the singing in my brain came to halt.

"The show is going to be called 'Musical!" Brad went on. "And the TV people are going to film everything—the rehearsals, the show— everything. And it's going to be way better than all those other high school musical shows because it's going to be all about us cool kids at Spenser."

"Braaaaaddd!" someone shouted.

"Just a minute there, Mr. Pierson."

The plaid jacket of Principal Eggars hovered beside Brad's arm (Brad's perfectly tanned, not-too-buff-but-tautly-muscled arm).

"The school's participation in the TV program is not a done deal," boomed Principal Eggars, a man who knew how to get the most out of a mike. "I only asked Brad to make the announcement today be- cause his father has been so instrumental in making the show a serious possibility."

A weighty pause followed as we all pictured a slightly greying, slightly heavier Brad-clone.

"I also wanted to assure you that if the program does go through, every effort will be made to avoid any disruption in your academic studies, which, as always, are the top priority here at Spenser."

Brad gave a big 'oh sure' kind of nod.

"Many details still need to be worked out by Mr. Pierson, Brad's *father*...and myself, of course. But if you have any immediate questions—"

Brad scooted his beautiful sun-bleached head to the mike again, "ask me."

"I guess that's right for the time being," Principal Eggars sighed.

"I love you, Brad!" came a wail.

Brad answered with another cute little wave.

Wow. I slowly closed my Bio notebook.

I love musicals. Yes, I sing them in my head, but I sing them out loud too. (Ask my older sister!) I am also a pretty good musical singer. (Her name is Maddy.) Not only because I've been practicing along with Julie Andrews, Bernadette Peters, and the Little Mermaid since age two (*Maddy'll* tell you), but also because I happen to have this really big singing voice. (Man, will she tell you!)

I don't like to brag, but I think I also have a pretty good singing voice. I had a chorus part in last year's musical, even as a lowly freshman, with a couple of solo lines too.

As Principal Eggars dismissed us and I waited for my row to move, I remembered how much fun last year's musical had been. My heart felt like dancing just thinking about it.

(*To laugh like a brook when it trips and falls...over stones on its way.*)

And then my dancing heart just tripped, only not like a laughing brook.

Because my heart was remembering something else about last year's show—the clips of it posted online after the first performance.

Which also made me remember Hank.

How could I forget Hank?

Hank was my nose, huge, curved, bulbous, pointed at the tip—the bane of my entire existence.

Okay, maybe not my *entire* existence, the bane of my existence for the last year.

It seems odd, I guess, but until I entered high school (actually, until I saw those clips of myself in last year's musical), I had never really thought much about Hank. Oh, I knew he...*it* was prominent. (My mom's word was "strong.") But that had never bothered me. Maybe because Hank was my dad's nose.

I was too young when my dad died to truly remember him, but when my mom and sister and I looked at old pictures or videos, it had always made me feel proud—*sad*, but proud—to have a nose almost exactly like his.

But after seeing those clips last year, everything changed. It was like a veil had been lifted from my eyes, or, maybe, my nose. I could suddenly see it clearly. How could I miss it? Hank was gi-normous.

As a free space opened in front of me, I straightened my backpack over my shoulders, trying to feel more positive.

(*I go to the hills...when my heart is lonely.*)

It was hard. Being on TV would be way worse than being on the Internet. TV cameras take close-ups. In focus. Women in those focused TV close-ups do not have Hanks in the middle of their faces, not even women in local weight loss commercials who have lost two hundred pounds and whose noses shouldn't matter.

A nose like mine would fit onto a TV screen about as well as an elephant's trunk would fit on a candy, one of those teeny round truffly ones.

I stared glumly around the auditorium. Brad was on the other side. Even on normal days, he stood out like a castle, male turret circled by girl moat. In the minutes since the announcement, the moat had swollen to a girl river, maybe even a girl sea.

The only bright spot on the horizon was Deanna, who waded straight towards me. (Deanna, who is both super tall and a little bit large around the middle, is not particularly fazed by girl moats.) Her hair was dyed silver blue to match a new book bag she carried. It looked like a bag she had made; duct tape crisscrossed its sides in a complicated geometric pattern. Deanna was big on duct tape.

Just now, random strands of hair clung to that duct tape, some straight and blonde, some curly and dark. I tried to let the sight of those hairs, which I was pretty sure were from Brad's girl moat, make me feel better.

(*My heart will be blessed with the sound of music.*)

I shook my head to get the song out.

(*And I'll sing...once...more.*)

So much for that.

(*Da daa da da daa.*)

II.

"Did you hear that the STC's going to let him cast it?" Deanna said, after we got out to the hallway.

The STC was the Student Theatre Council. It arranged all the shows at Spenser, picking the student producers and directors, who then controlled everything. (Teachers only vaguely supervised, mainly making sure people didn't stay too late in the building.)

"Brad? But he's never had anything to do with the musical. He doesn't even do plays."

"He's the one bringing in the TV crews."

"His dad," I sighed.

"Same difference," she shrugged.

Not really. Brad—Brad's dad. One had more Ds. But what was the point in arguing? If Brad's dad were setting it up, and Brad insisted that *he* was really in charge, no one on the STC would refuse him anything.

"So, you might only get in the chorus line," Deanna sighed. "Even the regular theater people give all the best parts to their friends."

I nodded, even though what Deanna said wasn't completely true. Of course, it helped to be best buds with the STC directors, but they did sometimes recognize, you know, *talent*.

"You could do a lot with a chorus part," Deanna went on.

"Sure," I sighed. "A chorus part would be great."

Then, a couple of periods later, I had real Chorus, the kind where you only sing, don't dance. (At Spenser, if you were in Chorus, you had it every day just like a class.)

There I was singing away with my very big, pretty good voice, when Ms. Deronda rapped me on the head with her baton. (Ms. Deronda was a great conductor, but nuts.)

"You've got to *blend* with the group, Pratchett!" she stormed. "Your voice stands out like a sore thumb...Make that a *big* thumb."

As my face flushed and my head stung, I wondered what kind of sound a thumb made. All I could come up with was the screech of someone being hit with a hammer.

"Singing in a chorus is about harmony. *Blending*!" Ms. Deronda went on. "And for Bach's sake," she turned wearily back to the group. "Is there anyone here who can accompany us until Lucinda comes back?"

Lucinda, our main student pianist, was on one of her multiple college tours. She was supposedly applying to twenty-five different schools. (All hail the Common App!)

"Speak up, folks! Can't a single one of you plunk yourself down over here?" Ms. Deronda gave a sharp nod towards the empty piano bench.

She was answered by a mixture of blank stares and searching glances. You had to play the piano really well to be an accompanist. Especially for a maniac like Ms. Deronda.

"I will guarantee an automatic A+ to whomever volunteers, plus 20 community service points. That's *if* you stick around as a regular substitute accompanist, *and* you're competent."

Some nudging among the baritones resulted in the slow half-raising of a hand. The boy it belonged to was a long lanky boy with long lanky limbs and longish lankyish hair.

I didn't know the boy's name. Only that he was a tall, quiet junior who was in a couple of my classes and almost always wore some kind of old rock and roll t-shirt. Today it read, "Cream."

He stepped down from the risers with the slightly stooped look of someone who had either (a) grown taller super fast, or (b) spent a lot of time hunching over something. I hoped, for his sake, that it was a piano and not a computer game.

Ms. Deronda studied her conductor's name chart. "Mr. Besss-eerrr-a?"

The tall boy shrugged.

"You play?"

"Sort of."

Ms. Deronda smiled sarcastically. "I guess we're going to have to hope you're also *sort of* modest."

With a small smile of his own, the boy sat down at the piano.

Ms. Deronda directed her chin back to me. "And you, Celia. What are you going to do?"

"Blend," I whispered.

I tried to smile, but tears pooled behind my eyes. Because there went me "doing a lot with a chorus part" in the televised musical. Brad was sure to hear about my blending problem. There were plenty of lala-ing mouths that would be eager to tell him come audition time.

Celia! Get a grip! There are more important things in the world than getting a part in a high school musical! What about droughts, floods, earthquakes, civil wars? That was the kind of stuff Maddy got upset about.

The problem was that getting a part in the musical was *very* important in my world, my personal world, one of the most important things there was.

But if I didn't keep the tears in, Hank would not only be huge, but red and snotty. That was the last thing I needed in any world.

III.

I don't know exactly what made me get so crazed over musicals. Partly, I guess, it's my voice. Partly, it's my mom.

My mom is kind of strict about certain things. Well, mainly education. She saves up all our money (not much) to send us to Spenser, a kind of expensive private school, because she thinks it's super academic. I get financial aid (Maddy did too when she was there), but Spenser is still a big stretch.

When we were little, my mom only let us watch TV programs and videos that she thought would teach us something. For some reason, musicals fit into that category—musicals, nature shows, and documentaries.

I liked animals as much as the next kid, and I did sometimes learn things from the documentaries, but pretty soon they both lost out to the best of Broadway. (I mean, how many times can you watch a panda sneeze? Well, a lot. But not, finally, as many times as *West Side Story*, or *Oliver!* or *The Sound of Music*.)

The Sound of Music was my favorite for a long time. It's a movie that is really dramatic for a little kid (the stern Captain, the cheating Baroness, the Nazis). I'm also a sucker for Julie Andrews. She's cute and perky and has an answer for almost everything. And, of course, she's got a totally fabulous voice.

That may be why I thought of her so much the day of Brad's announcement. What kept popping into my mind was Maria, when she's a nun, saying that God never shuts a door unless he opens a window. Which means, I guess, that you should never give up on what you truly want, no matter what.

So, even as Hank seemed to slam a great big door on my hopes during Chorus, someone opened a window for me later that day. If it was God, He/She took the form of my math teacher.

Ms. Geller is totally geeky. For one thing, she's studying to be a lawyer at night; this makes her harder for most kids to follow than even the average Spenser math teacher.

At the beginning of Pre-Cal, she cleared her throat loudly: "as I have been compelled to mention several times heretofore, class, and as I am sure you will all bear witness, there is altogether too much bilateral conversation during our sessions—conversation which, I must assume, is not limited to the subject of integers. Accordingly, as of today and henceforward, you will each take seats of *my* choosing, rather than your own."

It took two whole minutes for the groaning to begin.

I groaned a little too even though I didn't really care where I sat. For some strange reason I'm pretty good in math and I was the only sophomore in that class. The rest were juniors and seniors, and I wasn't close friends with any of them. Still, when Ms. Geller began calling out names, I paid close attention. What I wanted to see was where she would put Brad Pierson.

As I watched Brad take his assigned seat, I noticed that his nose was nicer than I had ever realized: it was absolutely perfectly straight.

Then guess who got the seat right next to him?

Thank *you*, Ms. Geller!

I tried to plop my stuff onto the desk with something that could be mistaken for grace.

"Hey!" Brad whispered. "Who are you?"

"Celia Pratchett." I cringed.

"Brad Pierson," he smiled, his brilliant teeth flashing like a camera on no-red-eye (intensely, slowly, repeatedly). Then he reached over to shake my hand. It was a gesture that seemed totally corporate until I looked into his gray-flecked hazel eyes, eyes that were *so* grey, *so* hazel, and *so* flecked that they made me wonder whether he wasn't secretly a profound person.

"Why don't I know you?" he asked.

(Because I have a hideous nose, I'm not super-popular, and I try to stay away from girl moats?)

"Maybe, um, because I'm a sophomore?"

"A sophomore in Pre-Cal, whoa!"

I blushed.

"So you must be a math genius." He nodded appraisingly.

I laughed. "I'm okay."

"Nice to meet you, Celia." He reached over again, squeezing my too-warm-and-sweaty fingers between his nice-and-cool dry ones.

"Numbers," Ms. Geller said sternly. "Remember, class, we are preparing, ultimately, for the Calculus. Let integers inform your every thought."

Oh, sure.

IV.

(People, people who need people—)

The second open-windowy thing that happened that day was actually an idea. Deanna's idea.

(Are the luckiest people—)

She had it at her place, which is where we almost always went after school.

(In the world.)

We'd walk through Washington Square, stop at Deanna's dad's cheese store, then, cheese and bread in hand, end up at Deanna's.

Their house was a super rad townhouse. Deanna's dad, who owned both the cheese store and a guitar store about a block away, seemed to have made a lot of money back in his younger days as a manager of a bunch of different rock bands. Her mom had been this glitzy fashion model, so I guess she'd also done pretty well for herself.

(We're children, needing other children—)

Deanna and I didn't feel much like children most of the time. But we did kind of feel that way when we sat in her mom's dressing room late afternoons. It was totally sunny and we would spread out a big striped beach towel to catch crumbs. Then we'd lie on it eating our baguette and cheese.

Deanna's family *called* it a "dressing room," but it was as big as a bedroom, with a long settee, two walls of mirrored closets, an old-fashioned Martian-headed hairdryer, and a dressing table crowded with greasy jars of face cream and assorted blow dryers. On the floor were stacks of old Vogues.

That afternoon we were pigging out on Brie.

Still, we weren't very happy.

Maybe this was why *People,* a kind of whiney song sung by Barbra Streisand in *Funny Girl,* was going through my head. That and because I was staring at Hank in one of the mirrored closet doors. Deanna knelt in front of another mirrored door, plucking her eyebrows.

"I'm never going to get a part in that stupid televised musical," I groaned. "Who ever heard of a TV singer with a Hank?"

Deanna, wrinkling her forehead, did not even look at me. "What about Barbra Streisand?"

It was like she was hearing my mind.

"Barbra Streisand got famous a long time ago," I said. There's no one like that now."

"Lady Gaga's nose is kind of big—"

"No, it isn't."

"How about Madonna?"

"Her nose isn't like mine. Anyway, Madonna's also got, you know—" I looked down at my chest. My breasts would fill a cone bra about as well as unfrozen yogurt.

"So what about…um…." Deanna pluck-pluck-plucked to gain time.

"You'd better come up with someone fast or you'll have a unibrow all on one side."

"There's that opera singer." Deanna re-wedged herself against the mirror to attack her other brow. "Maria something. My dad made me listen to old clips of her online."

"Opera singer?"

We both pretended to think for a minute, but neither of us knew much about opera singers. Anyway, I didn't want to sing in an opera. What I wanted was to sing in a musical. And musical stars had pert, cute little noses. Like Julie Andrews and Bernadette Peters and the Little Mermaid.

"Hey, I know!" Deanna's voice brightened. "Maybe you could get it fixed."

"Fixed?"

"Plastic surgery!"

"Before the auditions?"

"They're not for a few months, right? Everybody's just talking about them now because of the TV stuff. Come on, let's look it up." Grabbing one more bite of bread crust (Deanna loved crust), she jumped from the towel.

(*A feeling deep in your soul—*)

"But—" I started.

(*Says you were half now you're whole—*)

"*But* if you want to actually do it," Deanna interjected, "you should first talk to my mom. Her old model friends get fixed all the time— face lifts, Botox, boob jobs. She probably even knows someone who'd give you a discount."

The mention of moms filled my chest with dread. My mom was very different from Deanna's mom. And it wasn't just my mom I was worried about.

At my place—which was a teeny apartment and a *whole* lot different than Deanna's house—people, i.e. my mom and sister—would not only think a nose job was unnecessary and unaffordable, but also bad for the planet. They'd probably even complain about the amount of electricity used in the operating room.

(*No more hunger and thirst*—)

Operating room!

More dread squeezed in, this time from the base of my stomach, until I caught my reflection, the mirrored row of my reflections—Hank times ten.

(*But first be a person who needs*—)

I thought of Brad—that perfect chiseled profile, those profound gray-flecked eyes.

"You really think they might give a discount?"

V.

The problem might have been the word "rhinoplasty." All it means is "nose job." The difference is that "nose job" sounds sort of necessary, even positive, like *repair job* or *getting a job,* while "rhinoplasty" sounds like poachers, hacksaws, poor dead mounds of endangered leathery flesh.

The word coated Deanna's computer screen that afternoon: Beverly Hills *Rhinoplasty*. Beverly Hills II *Rhinoplasty*. Beverly Hills III *Rhinoplasty*.

"Aren't there any in New York City?"

"Of course." Deanna clicked a link to 'Park Avenue Rhinoplasty.'

"All types of aesthetic surgery," the site said.

"*Aesthetic* surgery?" I asked.

"Like art," Deanna said.

The screen filled with "before" and "after" pictures. Long noses becoming short noses. Thick noses, thin. Bumped, straight.

"They do guys, too?"

"Sure, but who looks at guys' noses?" Deanna shrugged.

I do. I look at everyone's noses. But I was too distracted by the words below the pictures to say anything. They were what you might call 'troubling' words: *"breaking...packing...splints...."*

"Scars...trouble breathing...straws...."

Straws?

I narrowed my eyes, trying to blur everything except for the occasional number—'let integers inform your every thought.'

"'Fourteen,'" I read aloud.

"Fourteen what? Oh. *'Bruising and swelling resolve itself in most patients in 14 days,'*" Deanna read aloud.

I turned from the screen.

"Would your mom let you take off from school?" Deanna asked, still scrolling through the website.

"No way."

"Maybe you could do it over Christmas."

A sleigh-line of miniature reindeer pranced through my brain, led by Rudolph's red bulb. "Don't think so," I sighed. My mom was the kind of person who really liked Rudolph.

"What if you told her it was your one chance to get on TV?"

"She hates TV."

"She let your sister be on TV."

"Not exactly 'let.'"

Maddy *had* been on TV a few times, but only when she was being arrested.

"Can't you tell her she's being unfair?" Deanna said. "That's what I always say. You know all the crap my folks buy the twins." Deanna had younger twin brothers, who, luckily, were out at organized sports most afternoons. "I tell them, look, don't I deserve something for a change?"

"Maybe," I whispered.

VI.

There's a really sweet song in *The Music Man* that I sometimes think of when I think about my mom: *there were bells on the hill, but I never heard them ringing, no, I never heard them at all....*

The catch is that if there were bells ringing on any hill, even a hill miles away, my mom would probably hear them.

My mom's got X-men level hearing.

This is not a great thing in New York City, which is not a very quiet place. It's even worse where we live, the West Village, a neighborhood of small, echoing streets that people like to roam at night, often after drinking heavily.

Some Village apartments may be quiet: apartments looking out over a garden, let's say, or sitting on top of a funeral home. Ours, unfortunately, is not one of them. It's partly over a pizza parlor, partly over a Lebanese deli, sort of catty-corner above a bar. It is also—just our luck—on the side of our building that faces the rumbling, traffic-filled

Hudson Street, and not the side that looks out on the narrow, hushed Morton Street.

My mom not only has supernatural hearing; she has lately been obsessed by noise. Her obsession first led her into a heated battle with the bar downstairs. (That fight started when the bar introduced dancing.) My mom had just managed to make the bar's management get the bar thoroughly soundproofed when the deli turned up the volume (mainly at 3 a.m. when things got kind of slow).

Now it was the pizza parlor that seemed to be causing the trouble. It sat just below my bedroom, and, every once in a while, made all my clothes smell like tomato sauce.

To make sure she had the right culprit, my mom kept coming into my room and getting down onto her hands and knees, one ear pressed to the floor.

This was not conducive to conversations about nose jobs.

I still tried. I geared myself up mentally by looking for a new Facebook profile picture. The one I had now was of me at age 10, dressed up as Dorothy for a little kid's production of *The Wizard of Oz*. I'd always thought the picture was sort of cute, but I could see (now that I finally had a brain), that I looked like a Dorothy with a carrot in the middle of her face.

"It *is* them!" my mother cried. "When I called, they said it must be a car, a woofer."

She pushed herself up from the floorboards. "Who do they think they're kidding?"

"Mom, it's not that bad."

"Can't you hear that bass?"

"Probably. If I pressed my ear to the floor."

I actually could hear the bass even without my ear pressed to the floor; it was a low *boom boomdiddy* below everything we said and did. But I didn't want to encourage her.

"Woofer," my mom muttered, standing at the computer now.

I pushed away from the computer. "Can we just go into the living room?" I tried. "I really need to talk to you."

"How are you ever going to get to sleep with all that racket?"

"Mom, it's only 8:30."

"Wait. I've got an idea. Why don't you come downstairs with me?"

"I totally don't want to stand there while you complain."

"I'm not going to complain. I'll just take a listen. You can pick up a slice."

"I don't like their slices. And I've got work to do. And I really really really need to talk to you."

"Please."

I groaned, but got my jacket. (*There were birds in the air, but I never saw them winging—*)

(*And there was music!*)

Okay, so there was music. There was always music. And maybe, if I could just get my mom to let me have my nose done, my life would have other kinds of stuff too. Like a decent profile picture.

I followed my mom into the stairwell—

(*And there were wonderful roses…they tell me—*)

—out onto Morton Street, then around the corner to Hudson, the sky darkening, the sidewalk dim.

(*In sweet fragrant meadows of dawn…and dew.*)

I sniffed the familiar scent of tomato sauce while my mom positioned her ear on the glass store-front window just over the stenciled words "Sal's Pizza"—

"Mom, I'm going upstairs."

"Celia, please," she protested, stepping back from the glass. "They may recognize my voice."

"You mean they may realize you're that nutty woman from upstairs?"

"Stay positive."

We pushed into a more vinegary smell—warmed-over bread dough. No wonder the slices weren't great. And yes, there was music, something disco-esque.

But it wasn't actually that loud.

The bass *was* a little insistent—the melody barely peeked over the drum beat. But it definitely wasn't deafening.

My mother's eyes, confused, searched the counter, the walls, the oven—

The pizza guy nodded, the cue for our order.

I went to the refrigerator case, got two bottles of water, took them to the counter.

"Aha!" my mom nudged, staring pointedly upwards. A small boom box was crammed onto a teeny shelf right above the soda machines, about two inches from the ceiling—

I paid the pizza guy, dragged my upturned mom to one of the small wooden tables.

"It's not the volume; it's where they've got it sitting," she whispered. "Celia, I know. Ask him to move it down."

"I can't buy two waters and ask him to move the boom box. Besides, they've got all the pizzas down there."

"So, ask him to turn down the bass."

"You ask him."

"Please Ceel. They already think I'm a nut case—"

"You *are* a nut case—"

"Please."

I wished (and not for the first time) that I was my sister. Maddy would either (a) just tell the guy to turn down the bass, because she truly believed that my mother's rights, as the upstairs residential tenant, were being infringed upon, or (b) tell my mom to shove it because she truly believed that the guy had every right in the world to listen to slightly loud music before 10 p.m. on weekdays. Either way, Maddy wouldn't just sit there, singing *Till There Was You* in her head.

I stepped back to the counter.

(*There was love all around*—)

"Would you mind…um…turning down the bass?" I said, pointing up to the boom box. "My mom's a little, you know, funny—" I circled my finger at the side of my head, the universal gesture for looniness, then felt a swish of air behind me. I turned, expecting to see my mom leaving in a small huff.

But my mom was still in her seat, staring up towards the ceiling. What had walked in the door was windswept blonde hair, a chiseled nose, and grey-flecked seriously profound eyes, which (thank God!) were not looking at me at just that moment.

I turned instantly back to the counter.

The pizza guy had propped a chair next to the soda machines. He stood on it reaching up to the boom box. "What you want?" he asked, looking down at me.

What I wanted was to sink through the floor.

"Lower?" the guy asked as the music dropped to a whisper.

"It's just the bass she wants lower."

"What you say?"

I refused to allow myself to look in Brad's direction, but I seemed to feel his presence, now to my left, at the refrigerator case.

"The bass," I tried again.

The pizza guy stared at me quizzically.

I prayed that Brad was too involved in the refrigerator to pay attention. "The bass," I repeated, trying to be make my voice both loud and deep but, at the same time, somehow soft, "the BASS."

As the music swung between whoosh and whisper, I watched Brad out of a corner of my hair.

Hey, wait a second. Brad didn't have his girl moat. This meant I could actually say *hi* to him. I could even remind him that he knew me from Pre-Cal.

He was taking out a beer.

A beer?

I gently shook my hair to get a better view. But now the beer bottle was no longer visible. It seemed—okay, I couldn't be absolutely sure—but it seemed to have gone under his tennis jacket.

"There's no bass control?" my mom asked, coming up to the counter.

"There just this one button." The pizza guy turned the volume control back and forth again with one large flour-dusted hand.

Cold air swept the space behind me. I knew, without looking, that Brad was gone.

(*No, I never heard them at all. . . .*)

The music—the *other* music (the stuff coming from the boom box)—was barely audible now.

Holding the soda machines for balance, the pizza guy stepped down from the chair, his face wearing the unmistakable flush of the hot and bothered.

"Thank you so much," my mom gushed.

The guy wiped his hands on his apron, then turned and went back to the kitchen.

"Oh dear," my mom moaned. "Am I absolutely terrible?"

I couldn't answer. All I could think of was that Brad had stolen a beer while we had distracted the pizza guy.

I tried to tell myself that I must be wrong, that I hadn't actually been paying attention to what Brad was doing.

Besides, maybe he had some kind of arrangement with the place; you know, because he was a minor and they weren't allowed to sell him beer.

So, he stole it?

Come on Celia. This is Brad you're talking about.

I didn't actually know what that meant.

As we climbed slowly upstairs, my mom's voice vacillated between triumph and guilt. I seemed to be stuck with the guilt part.

That's not totally accurate. What I was stuck with was Brad, his beautiful fingers grasping the beer bottle, his honey-tanned face, his announcement that he was in charge of the spring musical, and my absolute certainty that he was going to have a whole lot to do with casting.

"So *now* can we talk?"

VII.

"But sweetie pie, you have a perfectly nice nose," my mom protested.

"Oh sure. That's easy for you to say. If you had a great big Hank in the middle of your face—"

Oops.

It turned out that my mom had not heard my nose's nickname before.

"I'm sorry," I repeated a few times.

"Of course, I know it's Dad's name," I went on.

"I didn't mean to take it in vain, honestly."

"I'm totally sorry, Mom."

"Mo-om."

I suddenly switched from tearful to mad.

Maybe I shouldn't have named my nose after my dead dad. That still didn't mean that I should let it dominate my whole face, my whole life, that I shouldn't try to do something about it.

My mom acted like changing my nose in any way whatsoever was an even bigger insult to my dad's memory than naming it after him. It was like my nose was all my dad had given me to remember him by, all he'd given *anyone* to remember him by. It was like I shouldn't even blow it too hard.

"Maybe Dad would have *wanted* me to fix my nose," I protested. "Maybe he would have said,'great, someone in my bloodline finally has the sense to do something about this stupid...*protuberance.*'"

My mom stopped breathing.

"I'm sorry," I tried again.

We were quiet then for a long time. My mom has a thing for elephants; I stared at the Indian tapestry of one that hung over our sofa—its trunk all silver and gold—wondering if maybe that was why she was in so much denial about my schnoz.

"It's getting late," she exhaled at last. "Did they turn that boom box back up?"

She went into my bedroom. I followed.

"They did," she said grimly, not even bothering to kneel down on the floor.

"They'll close soon—"

"They'd better turn it off then. "

An orange light blinked at the bottom of my computer screen; I sat down to check it out.

Message for Bluesong. Chat request from Boymeetsgirl17. Do you accept?

Boymeetsgirl17?

Wait a second. There was a picture of Brad. Teeny, but with his perfect, knowing, tennis, surfing smile.

Bluesong: Yes!

Boymeetsgirl17: yo Ceel! Brad here. From Pre-Cal.

Did that mean he didn't notice me in the pizza parlor?

Boymeetsgirl17: I got your screen name from Mia in chorus.

I pictured a tall thin alto (one of Ms. Deronda's darlings), who took attendance and sent out emails before every concert telling us to make sure to wear a real white blouse (not a wifebeater), and not to gunk up our throats with dairy and chocolate. (For some reason, she always sent me two of these emails.)

Bluesong: hey!!!

Geez! What was me and exclamation points!?!!

Boymeetsgirl17: u finish math? She gave a ton, huh?

Bluesong: totally.

Lame.
But at least without exclamation points.

Boymeetsgirl17: cool. What'd u get for 1?

Bluesong: just a sec.

I rifled through the mess of papers in my bag, then typed out the answer.

Boymeetsgirl17: What about 2?

I typed out that answer.

Boymeetsgirl17: how about 3? Hey—u mind writing out the equations—so I can check my work—

We went on like this till I had given him all the answers, all the back-up work too.

I tried not to think about the beer, or the fact that I wasn't just "helping" him with math.

I tried to tell myself that no one was perfect.

I also tried to think of some way to bring up the musical.

Bluesong: so congrats about the TV thing.

Boymeetsgirl17: all is well all is fine talk to u some other time.

Away.

Damn.

VIII.

The next morning I wore an old plastic Groucho mask to breakfast, the kind with glasses, mustache, and fake nose.

My mom pretended not to notice.

I took it off before I went to school, but even off, I could feel the rub of plastic against Hank's sides. (In short, wearing the mask had no effect on my mom but made me feel even more deformed than usual.)

"She won't let me do it," I groaned to Deanna in homeroom.

Deanna wore a lavender camisole with a crocheted poncho on top to cover the bulges of skin around her bra top. Deanna was always very tasteful that way. She'd also put some new lavender streaks in her hair.

"Did you tell her it was the only way you'd get a part?"

"She just said, 'what about Barbra Streisand?'"

"She's got a point."

"Give me a break."

I tried all the rest of that day to come up with a winning argument. But it's hard to really think something through in school. The atmosphere just isn't right somehow.

In Pre-Cal, for example, there was Brad to attend to. He didn't exactly ooze gratitude for my help with his homework, though he did give me one of his cute little waves.

That was the extent of our direct contact. Still, Brad provided plenty of distraction. It wasn't just his nose that was perfect; his cheekbones showed at the sides; the tiniest cutest stubble hugged his chin.

Then he kept writing stuff in his notebook—not math stuff—stuff like "Pacific Tan at 5," and "Call Stephanie about directors being able to act." Next to the name 'Stephanie,' he drew a smiley face above two smaller one-eyed smiley faces.

Oops. So, not one-eyed smiley faces.

I turned quickly from the big-boobed sketch.

Chorus, at least, was better.

Yes, Ms. Deronda stopped mid-measure and smiled at me, making a stirring gesture. *But* she didn't hit me with the baton.

Actually, she was in a better mood than she'd been in all week. Mr. Bessera, who had on his "Cream" shirt again today, turned out to be a very good accompanist.

The only thing that bothered Ms. Deronda was that every time she took a break from conducting in order to lecture us, he seemed to go to sleep.

"Mr. Bessera!" she barked, when she was ready for the music to start again. Once she even banged the top of the piano.

All he did was open his eyes slowly, bring his hands back from behind his head, and begin to play again, precisely at the place she wanted.

Which took quite a bit of nerve, I thought.

Ms. Deronda couldn't exactly complain. Lucinda, our regular accompanist, hid drafts of her college essay in the sheet music and was way more confused starting up.

Mr. Bessera was in my gym class too, I realized. One of the doomed.

We'd gotten totally shafted in gym. In the first week of school we'd had Mr. Garth who was the hippest gym teacher in the school. Then Mr Garth broke his leg teaching the rollerblading elective, and Ms. Pavlova was brought in to torment us.

The boys at Spenser all called Ms. Pavlova a real ball buster. I don't know what she busted on girls, but what she did do was take lots and lots of points off people's grades: for lateness, for not having sneakers, or not having tieable sneakers or not having tied-up sneakers, for talking in class or texting in class (only then she'd actually confiscate your phone). At Spenser, your gym grade didn't count in your grade point average, but Ms. Pavlova took off so many points she'd fail you. And, as she frequently pointed out, Spenser high school students needed to pass eight semesters of gym in order to graduate.

We hadn't even gotten a third of the way through this particular semester and Deanna and I were already pushing it.

The problem was that Deanna's locker was a complete mess. Not her gym locker—we didn't have permanent gym lockers—her hall locker. Which was where I always stopped to meet her before gym.

"Do you know 'Cream?'" I asked as she picked through the stash that nearly came up to her waist.

She looked at me mid-duct tape. (She had just pulled out two rolls of it—bright orange and lavender.) "As in whipped?"

"As in some kind of band. This boy in Chorus always wears a t-shirt that says 'Cream.' He's in gym too. You know—that tall guy, kind of brown hair?"

"Tall guy, kind of brown hair?" Deanna wiped color onto her lips distractedly. Deanna loved color.

"Knobbly knees."

"Cream was a Brit band. In the 60s, I think, maybe 70s...uh, Eric Clapton."

"And he was?"

"This super great guitarist."

Deanna knew all about this kind of stuff from her dad; she'd been listening to vintage rock since babyhood.

"He's old, but still performs," she said thoughtfully. "Eric Clapton, I mean. He's like the world's greatest guitarist—blues, rock. He did, like, *Layla*, and then there was Derek and the Dominos."

"Cool," I said. Deanna was a great source of information, but once she got going, she was very hard to—

"Then 'Sunshine of your—'"

"Also," I jumped in, "do you know who in our class has had *you know*?" I leaned into the Pisa of duct tape.

Deanna lowered her voice. "I heard that Michael Lorton and that new girl Racine snuck below the bleachers right after sixth last week."

"Not *that* 'you know!' Plastic, I mean, *aesthetic* surgery."

"Oh." Deanna squeezed her locker closed—it took a couple of tries. "Jessica Villon, Emma Sizemore, and..." she sighed, "I *think*, Tracy Richards."

"Tracy? Seriously? Her nose is okay, but not great."

"Not nose, ears. Don't you remember fifth grade? Little Miss Dumbo." She waved her hands by the sides of her face.

"Oh yeah! But I totally loved her ears! I remember thinking how cool it was that she never needed a headband."

"To each her own," Deanna sighed.

IX.

We ran across the gym to get to the girls locker room; its entrance was way over on the far side. Just after we slipped through the blue-framed door, Ms. Pavlova locked it.

"Christ," Deanna muttered. "Isn't that against some fire code?"

"I think it's only locked on the outside." I gently pushed the door open. "See. It doesn't actually lock any one in."

"What a 'B*****,'" Deanna said. (We tended not to say the full word due to rigorous training from Maddy, who argued that society applied it to almost any strong woman.)

"Yeah," I agreed. "Come on."

We clambered through a forest of sleeves and legs, bare arms and legs too, to some empty lockers. From the corner of one eye, I could see Tracy Richards and Jessica Villon, already in gym clothes, angling in front of the mirror.

Tracy and Jessica were the kind of girls who wore cute little coordinated short sets. Only, to avoid excessive cuteness, the sets tended to be black or grey with a rumple of funkiness. Jessica had the word "pink" written over her behind.

I tried not to stare, but couldn't help myself, not now that I knew that Tracy and Jessica were both "fixed."

Was there any *bruising, swelling?* I was pretty sure that would have...*resolved* itself by now. And what about scars?

I tried not to make my stares obvious, but Jessica and Tracy, still in front of the mirror, wouldn't have noticed me if I'd taken out a telescope.

Their faces seemed absolutely perfect. Okay, there was one zit on Jessica's forehead, which she tried to smooth by manually stretching out the skin around it. But other than that, there were no more blemishes on either of them than a Barbie doll. (A new Barbie doll, not one that's been jammed in a car seat for five years.)

Even their legs were Barbiesque, hose-smooth, liposuction-firm.

And their noses—

Just as I was assessing their noses, Emma Sizemore bounced up to them. She had sleek black leggings under her cute little shorts.

I felt cloddier than ever. In my house, when it was a gym day, you just grabbed what you could find. (Actually, you grabbed what you could find on a gym day in early September and then kept it in your backpack until Christmas vacation or absolute rankdom, whichever came first.)

What I had found were old shorts of Maddy's. They were kelly green with bright white stripes down the side. I was pretty sure that Maddy had picked them up years ago from the middle school lost and found.

(Spenser had three schools right next to each other—lower, middle and high.) The shorts somehow managed to be both too puffy *and* too tight.

Deanna wore long satiny basketball shorts that had once belonged to her dad. She had made them her own by covering them with a jagged pattern of duct tape. (Weird, but cool, but also sort of, you know, *weird*.)

In other words, Deanna and I were not the belles of the gym class.

I looked at Emma's nose again. I vaguely remembered the old one as thick, long—not a true Hank, but almost. Now she seemed to be constantly wrinkling it.

Emma's lips were also suspicious. She was just then glossing what seemed to be a permanent pout.

I tried to remember what her old lips looked like, but lips just weren't the kind of thing you noticed in the third grade. That seemed to be the last time I'd paid close attention to Emma. I remembered one particular day back then when she was chosen captain of one of the kickball teams and had deliberately avoided picking both me and Deanna. (B****, I thought.)

(Come on, Celia! These are your friends! Kids you've known since lower school!)

"You ready?" Deanna said. I slunk out behind her feeling big-nosed, badly-dressed, incredibly disloyal, and terrible at kickball.

And who was out in the gym? Brad Pierson! Brad Pierson who didn't even have to take regular gym because he was captain of tennis team.

What was *he* doing there?

He stood with a dragonfly blue racket beside another team member. They had tied off a portion of the gym with neon green tape.

Brad sighed heroically, then went through the motions of a serve, which he slammed—boom!—into a side wall.

Tracy, Emma, and Jessica tittered over to the neon green tape.

"Hey Brad," Emma called through her idiotically pouty lips. "Looking good."

"Hi there," Brad said, with a quick thumbs-up.

Jessica chimed in with a "hi there" of her own, and Tracy—Tracy!— ran under the neon green tape, picked up the tennis ball, and tossed it to Brad. Totally unnecessary since it was rolling back towards him anyway. As Brad's hand clasped the ball, Tracy made a little 'whoo' sound. Brad grinned.

I immediately hated them all. That is, I hated Jessica, Emma and Tracy. But I reserved a special circle of hatred for Tracy, whose ears, I decided, looked like pancakes. Pancakes with earrings.

And she *did* have hose on under her shorts. The sheen caught the bright gym light as she minced back into our disheveled line-up.

Talk about idiotic. (And smooth.)

Jessica, Tracy, Emma waved at Brad in perfect unison. He, in turn, gave them an appraising look. Did it say, "chorus line?"

X.

All day I thought about Emma and Jessica's cute little sculpted noses, Tracy's flattened ears, their perfect gym shorts, pouts, and stupid little idiotic throws of Brad's tennis balls.

I didn't like them, and yet I was sure that they were somehow the key to my problems. Jessica, Tracy, and Emma…the perfect girls. (At least they thought so!)

It was only when I was at Deanna's that afternoon, drinking hot chocolate (a supertanked fuel for ideas), that the answer came to me: it was more or less your classic guilt trip.

Sure, it was mean. Especially to use on someone as susceptible as my mom, but what else did I have?

Here was the argument: that a nose job was something my mom would have been able to provide for me if we were a 'regular family.' Like Tracy's or Emma's or Jessica's.

Now, I personally don't know what exactly a regular family *is*. Or whether Tracy, Emma, or Jessica actually had one. But my mom is not me; she has certain ideas. She doesn't say it out loud, but secretly she believes that a regular family, a *good* family, the kind of family that everyone else at my overly-expensive private school must have, is a family with two living-together parents, two living-together parents who make a lot more money than she does.

Then, when my mom feels guilty about the one-parent-kind-of-broke family *we* have, she goes out and buys us something. Not a newer apartment, or a bigger apartment, or an apartment that is not right over a pizza parlor—all of that is impossible. Instead, she gets something small, but pricey, like a matching set of cashmere sweaters, some fancy pastries, maybe even tickets to a play.

Would a fixed nose qualify? It would be small—in size anyway. And pricey. A lot more than cashmere.

I groaned inside, the guilt trip already working, on me at least.

(*Sunrise, sunset. Sunrise, sunset. Swiftly fly the days.*)

That song is from *Fiddler on the Roof*. It's not a real belt-em-out number, but it has a wistfulness that's totally lovely.

I really felt that wistfulness on my way home from Deanna's that day. Maybe because it *was* sunset. Sunsets and wistfulness go together somehow like, you know, *tea, a drink with jam and bread*. (To quote another great song.)

Sunset on my street is especially tea with jam and bready. Morton Street is lined with trees and bottomed with cobblestones, and after one deep bend, you can see all the way to the Hudson River, crinkling and twinkling a couple of blocks away.

(*Sunrise, sunset.*)

I was at the edge of that bend and could just make out the shimmer that would take over the street once it turned fully towards the river.

If I could only inhale that glow, I thought. Then maybe I could speak glowingly about Tracy, Emma, and Jessica, about their perfect families too. I was pretty sure I would have to do that to successfully guilt-trip my mom.

But when I thought of perfect, and thought of guilt, my mind filled with Brad.

I thought of his hair and eyes, his smile and forearms. (Did tennis give him those great wrists? You know, with all the racket action?)

(*Swiftly fly the years.*)

What if I just got Brad really used to me doing his math homework? So dependent that he felt like he owed me something?

Maybe then I wouldn't *have* to guilt-trip my mom. Maybe then I wouldn't even need a nose job.

"Hey, Miss, watch yourself."

I looked up to a guy wearing a complicated vest—the kind with eight different tool pockets—and down at a web of black cables. There was a large silver van parked at my side, a movie van.

There was another movie crew guy further down, covering the cables and the rest of the sidewalk too, with red plastic leaves scattered from a couple of huge plastic garbage bags.

Another guy was on a stepladder that leaned against one of the Sycamore trees lining the block. He was tying fake leaves on the branches with little striped baggie ties. He had already tied these fake leaves on several other trees, the little striped ties glinting in the sunlight.

As I stepped over the cables, I studied the plastic leaves. They were way bigger and floppier than the real leaves. They were also a bright veiny red. (The real ones were yellow, edged with brown and green.)

"What are you filming?" I asked the vest guy.

"A movie," he said as he tried to push a plastic stick with more leaves on it between the cracks in the pavement. "Called uh... 'Last Autumn in New York.'"

(*One season following another—*)

For a second, I wanted to laugh. I mean, right now was *this* autumn in New York and here was this film crew, putting fake plastic leaves all over the place.

(*Laden with happiness and—*)

But the next instant I felt so low—

(*tears...*)

—that I couldn't even manage any decent New Yorker smugness. If even beautiful trees and leaves had to be "fixed" to be on film, what about someone like me? Someone who wasn't beautiful at all.

Doing Brad's homework just didn't feel like enough.

XI.

My mom was home when I got in. Great.

And the boom boxes—I quietly put my head to the floor—were off downstairs.

Even better.

But then I heard from my mom's room: "Darling, I really don't think you should go out to Nevada during your break."

She was speaking in her worried voice, worried-bordering-on-terrified. That could only mean one thing.

I quietly picked up the extension.

"It's not like I'm going to Las Vegas, Mom," Maddy protested at the other end of the line. "I'm not going to be a show girl or gamble or—"

"Protesting nuclear warheads isn't a gamble, Maddy—you're almost guaranteed to end up in jail."

"We're not going to *do* anything to the warheads."

"Trying to get *near* them is bad enough."

"Mom," Maddy groaned. "I've *got* to try to do something. It's who I am! it's why I'm on this planet—"

"Can't you—oh, I don't know," my mom sighed. "Can't you just get yourself a nice boyfriend?"

"Mom! That is *so* prehistoric. Anyway," Maddy chuckled, "I *have* a nice boyfriend."

I could feel the birth of my mom's hope even through the extension.

"Surely, *he* doesn't want you to sneak around nuclear warheads," my mom said.

"His name is Terry and he's planning to come with me."

Newborn hope crumpled into age-old despair. "Maddy," my mom whispered. "I'm not going to be able to bail you out of a federal crime. Not with everyone worrying about terrorism."

Feeling sick and sorry—well, mainly sick and irritated—I put down the phone.

So maybe I was being selfish. All I could think about was how impossible it was going to be to make my mom *feel guilty* when my sister was in danger of being *found guilty*. My mom was definitely not going to shell out big bucks for cosmetic surgery if she thought she had to save up every single penny for Maddy's legal defense fund.

I heard my mom hang up. I looked in the door of her teeny bedroom.

A big part of me was furious with her—I mean, who strolled Maddy and me to our first demonstration up in midtown? (I still remember the pretzel carts reflecting the gleam off the U.N. tower.)

And who, when we were older, was so proud of Maddy's petitions? Against sweatshops, land mines, tobacco ads, guns, arctic drilling, sports that excluded women.... (I had stopped keeping track some time ago.)

Who went with Maddy to get those petitions signed when she was too little to wander the streets by herself? And who insisted on dragging me along when I was too little to be left home by *myself*?

Who, when Maddy was obsessed with animal rights, not only didn't make her wash her hair, but bought her a ton of organic hair care products, trying for weeks to convince her that the company truly didn't test on animals when the bottles had that little rabbit with the line through it?

And who, even when she picked Maddy up at the police station, never really yelled at her? (At least not in front of the cops.)

My brain was full of reasons why Maddy's craziness was all my mom's fault, and I was about to list them loudly one by one. Then I saw my mom sitting on her bed, her head in her hands.

Who can kick a puppy when it's down?

Okay, so my mom isn't a puppy. You get the idea.

I squeezed in beside her. She put her arm around me, grateful, I guess, that she had *one* daughter who wasn't checking out airfares to Las Vegas.

"I could try writing her," I said.

"Would you?"

"And maybe we could—I don't know—come up with a different cause."

"Now, there's an idea."

"I'll get Deanna to look too."

My mom blew her unfairly beautiful nose. "That would be wonderful."

While Deanna searched from her computer at her house, I looked from ours. My mom paced behind me, going through all our charitable mailings.

(*Before the parade passes by....*)

That song is from *Hello Dolly!* I somehow always think of it when it comes to Maddy.

(*Before it goes on and only...I'm left.*)

It's the way she just kind of dominates things in my family, even when she's not at home.

(*Before the paraaade passes by....*)

My mom was looking into really tame alternatives, like get-out-the-vote drives. "She's got to have seen the difference that kind of work makes," she said.

Bluesong: my mom wants her to get out the vote.

Pinkwstripes: didn't they do that already?

"She probably won't go for that," I said over my shoulder.

(*I gotta get in step while there's still time left.*)

Pinkwstripes: how about penguins?

Bluesong: penguins?

Pinkwstripes: I like penguins. And remember that time Maddy's hair got so dirty?

No one ever forgot that time Maddy's hair got so dirty.

Bluesong: penguins actually sound pretty good.

Pinkwstripes: penguins r great.

(*I'm ready to move out in front.*)

I was just following up on penguins when Maddy herself came online.

Bluesong: you!

Madabout1: hey girl! How goes it back in NYC?

Bluesong: not good. You're freaking out Mom, you know that don't you?

Madabout1: she told you?

Bluesong: she's freaking out.

Madabout1: people *should* freak out. We're talking about the proliferation of really dangerous weaponry.

Bluesong: can't you just write some letters?

Madabout1: Ceel!

Bluesong: your new boyfriend isn't making you do this?

Madabout1: boys don't MAKE me do anything.

Bluesong: sorry. I mean, is he really into it?

There was a long silence.

A LONG silence.

Which could have meant that she was writing someone else, or getting up to pee, *or* that the boyfriend wasn't all that into Maddy's Nevada scheme either.

Bluesong: what's his name again?

Madabout1: Terry

(I've had enough of just passing by life.)

Bluesong: is he nice?

Madabout1: he plays the cello.

Suddenly, something snapped inside me. I don't know what it had to do with cellos except that they seemed somehow so *civilized,* while my sister seemed so nutty—not because she was against nuclear war—but because she planned to protest it in a way that probably wouldn't get that much attention but would still land in her prison (while also making our mom bankrupt.)

And she had a boyfriend! Who played the cello! And who was probably a really nice guy!

I mean, here I was, with not one single boyfriend my whole life, without even the hope of a boyfriend, all because of a stupid nose that Maddy was now keeping me from getting fixed because her favorite form of political speech was getting arrested.

(*With the best of them, with the rest of them,*

I wanna hold my head up high.)

I'm probably not explaining it right. All I can say is that I was p.o.ed.

Bluesong: Maddy, come on. There's got to be something you and Terry can do that won't drive mom off the deep end.

As I waited for a response, the orange light started blinking at the base of my screen again. Boymeetsgirl17.

I sighed but didn't answer. I didn't want let up on Maddy for one second right now even if she wouldn't be able to tell.

(*For I've got a goal again, I've got a drive again.*)

Madabout1: sigh. Terry wants to volunteer on a weather boat for a few weeks, taking water temperatures, measuring the speed of ice floe melts, all that kind of stuff.

Bluesong: and practicing the cello?

Madabout1: ha!

Bluesong: that sounds really cool. Maybe you could save some penguins.

Madabout1: we'd go North, silly. But it'd be expensive. A lot more than Nevada. I could cover Nevada out of my own money.

Bluesong: not your legal fees.

Madabout1: ha!

Ha again? Geez.

Bluesong: seriously, Mads, talk to Mom.

Blink blink blink blink went the little orange light. My fingers itched—I mean, even if he did just want homework, he was still Brad.

Madabout1: she's really upset, huh?

Bluesong: Duh!

Madabout1: ok, ok, I'll call her.

Bluesong: Thanks!

Madabout1: Luv you!

I typed out the fastest "luv you back" in history and then checked on that little orange light.

Brad had been busy.

Boymeetsgirl17: yo, Ceel.

Boymeetsgirl17: helloooooo?

Boymeetsgirl17: prettyplease!

Boymeetsgirl17: ur not holding out on me?

What was it Maddy had said about not letting boys MAKE her do anything?

But it was easy for Maddy. Maddy, with my mom's perfect nose, Maddy, who never cared about anything except land mines, nuclear warheads, the length of my showers, and now, I guess, melting ice floes.

I was not Maddy.

(*I wanna hold my head up high.*)

Bluesong: sorry. You need 4?

Boymeetsgirl17: Yeah, 4 & the others too, huh

As I typed answers, my mom gushed behind me, back on the phone with my sister. "Oh, Maddy, that's so terrific. Climate change is something that affects the whole planet."

As if nuclear warfare wasn't, I pouted silently.

"Of course, I'd be glad to pay for part of it," my mom went on.

Man, life was unfair.

(*Before the paraaaaaade...*)

Hey, wait a second....

(*...passes by.*)

XII.

"So what you're telling me, Mom, is that you'll do practically *any-thing* to keep Maddy out of one short little prison term, while you'll do absolutely *nothing* to help me out of the lifelong dominion of this stupid honker?"

I pointed at Hank. My mom rolled her eyes (for about the zillionth time), but I was sure I was making headway. She was quiet now, not groaning, not yelling, not getting down on the floor. (I prayed that they'd keep the boom box off downstairs.)

"Okay, Celia," she said at last. "I'll give you my legal consent for a nose job if you want it so much. I'm not saying that it's a good idea, mind, or that you need it, or that it even makes any sense. But if you earn the money for the surgery yourself, and I mean *earn*—"

"You're paying for part of Maddy's weather trip."

"That's educational."

"The musical's part of school."

"Celia—" my mom started. But what could she say?

She shook her head; she sighed again. "I'll give you the same amount I'm giving Maddy for her trip. But keep in mind, sweetie, that doesn't mean I think you should do it."

"I know Mom, you're all for Barbra Streisand."

"She's had a great career."

There were conditions. (There always are.) My mom typed up a little contract to make these perfectly clear.

"It has to be a reputable surgeon," she insisted. "No skimping on the medical part."

I nodded.

"And you can't have a job that interferes with your schoolwork."

"What if it's a really well-paying job?"

She bent over the little contract. "No job that interferes with your schoolwork, *your physical well-being, or,*" she scribbled in the margin, "*your moral character.*"

"Mom! I'm not going to become a hooker."

"I didn't say you would."

"Or sell drugs."

"Of course not, sweetie."

"But you're not going to make me quit just when I've almost earned enough—"

"I hope you know I'm a fair person."

"Just say you won't."

Her face reddened. "I won't."

After my mom and I signed the contract, I ran to Deanna's.

Deanna jumped up and down so much as she hugged me that I almost felt insulted. (Deanna had always insisted that Hank wasn't that bad.)

Then we looked through her mom's old Vogues, happily picking my new nose. (I mean, picking *out* my new nose.)

I tended to go for small. But Deanna dismissed all the small ones as "too cute" or "too Emmafied."

"If you're going to take the trouble," she said, "you've got to go for *beautiful*. Like this one. Narrow, straight, elegant." She stared at me, then back to the page. "She's got your face shape, see."

I looked down at the pale, slender face, which was totally beautiful even though the model seemed to be sneering at the whole world. It was hard to feel like I had much in common with a face like that.

"So, when?" Deanna asked. "You have to wait till Christmas vacation?"

"I can't actually schedule it yet. I have to earn the money first."

"Celia! No way!"

"Come on, Dee," I said, trying to ignore the tragedy in her voice. "I can get a job on weekends, maybe after school."

"Wait. I've got it. Maybe you could borrow the money from my folks."

"No loans."

She looked at me quizzically.

"That's one of my mom's rules."

"Bummer.... So, then, maybe—maybe you could get someone to write you up in a magazine or something—the kid who's paying for her own nose job. And then," Deanna laughed, "the magazine could pay for it."

"Maybe," I said doubtfully. "But wouldn't they only write about me if I were the kid *paying* for her own nose job."

"Oh yeah." Deanna's face fell. "Right."

We stared at the glossy page. The model's sneer now seemed to be directed at me personally, just like another Tracy, Emma or Jessica, or any other perfect girl.

I'll show you, I thought.

XIII.

"$1200 AN HOUR!!! AND UP!!!!" the ad said. (I know, I know. You shouldn't believe everything you read on the Internet.)

I actually *hadn't* believed it. But I *had* been dumb enough to think that if the ad said $1200, I might be able to earn at least $300. At $300 an hour, I figured that I could get Hank fixed by Christmas, even just working part-time.

I hurried home after school, put on some interview clothes (sneaking one of my mom's old blazers), found my social security number, wrote it on my arm, pulled my sleeve over it, then headed out. I took the bus up Hudson Street since the address was so far west. It was blocks from the nearest subway, way over by the Lincoln Tunnel.

Got off in a really hideous part of the City, the streets clogged with bumper-to-bumper traffic, the buildings dingy with exhaust. The shops seemed to be locksmiths mainly, iron bars coating their windows, small neon keys overhead.

Found the address at a faded brown block of a building. The lobby did not bode well. The woodwork was corroded, the linoleum cracked. Flaking wallpaper bore a pattern of little golden keys.

(What was this thing with the keys?)

A security guard sat with his feet propped on a battered desk, an old staticky radio scratching the air. One of those short-paged newspapers lay in front of him, open to blurred photos of football players in uniforms, girls in bikinis.

"Soft Soap Cosmetics?" I asked.

He looked me up and down in a way that made me wish I'd worn a bulky sweater, then flicked his head towards an ancient elevator. "Fifth floor."

The elevator had a metal cage door just behind its main door. A very short man in a way oversized red jacket nodded as I stepped inside.

"Five," I said. The elevator man pulled the inner metal cage door shut, the heavy outer door following squeakily, then pressed the "5" button a couple of times. When nothing happened, he banged a place below the buttons where all the paint had worn off.

As the elevator grumbled upwards, I tried to imagine that five was my lucky number.

(*'Five golden rings,'* my brain sang out helpfully.)

The elevator swayed to a stop. The little man creaked open both sets of doors, then jerked his head towards the right.

There were several doors in the dim hallway, which was definitely not a golden ring kind of place.

The door that belonged to Soft Soap Cosmetics had deep gashes in the jamb. I tried to view the gashes as hopeful signs, as if they meant there was something in there worth burglarizing.

There was also a row of other signs—the kind made of plastic—that ran down the center of the door. It was a maroon door, the thick sick color of surgical scrubs.

The thought of surgical scrubs made me shiver inside. (*'Swelling and bruising resolve themselves in most patients in 14 days.'*)

I tried to settle down, to focus on what the signs actually said.

The top one: "Soft Soap/Saddle Soap/ Cosmetics, Inc."

The next: "Wearable Warranties Limited."

Then: "Clean Up Your Credit Corp."

Finally: "Wash Your Mouth Out LLC."

This did not, somehow, look like the door to an office where people made even just $300 dollars an hour.

I almost turned back down the hall, but I couldn't bear to face the elevator guy again so quickly. I made myself knock.

No answer.

The thought that no one was there made me feel good enough to knock a second time, louder.

"Come in already," a voice yelled. "Whaddya waitin' for?"

With palpitating heart, I pushed open the heavy door. It was like one of those cartoons where a character flips open a box and a roar of noise pours out, then he shuts the box and the noise stops, then he opens it and it starts all over again.

Only it wasn't noise so much as words.

"Is this Mrs. Courbe... Courbe...Courbitor—That's not how you say it?—"

"You're 80? Well, it gets rid of wrinkles too."

"Ooh baby, ooh yes, I've got you yeah, so tight—"

"Please, man, hear me out. You got warts? Come on now, everybody's got warts."

"Important news about your car's warranty...."

There was a desk in the center of the room that was as big as a counter. Behind it were a couple of aisles of cubicles, some covered by curtains, some open. I could see people sitting in the open ones—an Asian woman in frayed jeans, an older lady in an African print dress, a geeky-looking guy thumbing a small video game gadget. He, like some of the others, had a headset on. Red lights lit on what looked like huge old phone consoles.

No one seemed to notice my entrance except, finally, a bald guy who sat at the front desk with a headset clamped over his yellowing scalp, a thick cigar in his fist. He waved the cigar towards me.

"Lady," he said as I came closer. "Did you know that your car warranty is about to expire? Yep, you are on our list, ma'am, and if you don't act fast—lady—hey, lady—you say you don't have a car—"

He pushed some buttons on the phone.

"It's me again. Yeah—Larry. Sorry about that. It's not our car list you was on, it's about your debt. Did you know, ma'am, that you are drowning?"

The line about drowning seemed apt somehow, though the room was stale, dry, and smelled of cigar. Maybe because his stomach was shaped like a beach ball.

The guy, Larry, pulled off the headset, shaking his head in a way that showed the tight squeeze of flesh crowding his chin, then turned to me. "And you are?"

"You want my name? It's, um, Celia Pratchett. I saw your ad, you know, for a job."

"Interested in Soft Soap, huh? Or Wash Your Mouth Out?"

He took a draw on the cigar, eyes narrowing.

"It said people could work part time," I tried.

"You can work evenings, right? 'Cause evenings are best in our line of work, see. You want to catch people at home."

"You call people at home?"

"That's right. We give you their numbers and then you call 'em and sell 'em things, sometimes soap, sometimes car warranties, sometimes," he shrugged, "debt."

"You sell people debt?" I asked. "Over the phone?"

"How do you usually call people?" Then, with a distracted frown, he stretched. This caused a triangle of hairy belly flesh (eeuw) to poke right through the buttons of his shirt.

I tried to look away. I tried to look as if I was gazing anywhere other than at that triangle of hairy flab. Okay, so the guy's got a gut, I told myself.

"You gotta learn stuff about 'em too," he said.

Oh geez. He was scratching it now.

"Even if they don't want to buy nuthin', you just sort of talk to 'em, ask 'em questions. It's like doin' a friggin' survey."

I wanted to ask him how you made the $1200 an hour, except that the whole thing suddenly seemed totally impossible—

"Then you make a commission, see. $10 to $15 per form, depending on how much you fill out. You get a percentage too, of the products. We also got a business here where people call us. But," he stared at the lapels of my blazer—actually, what he stared at was my chest. "I think we should just start you with sales."

His upper lip tightened around a piercing whistle.

I jumped. No one else even budged.

"Louise!" he shouted.

A tall thin girl with teased hair and heavy make-up came out from one of the cubicles.

"I'm on break."

"This girl here—"

"Celia," I supplied.

"Celia. I'm Larry, by the way. Celia here needs a horn and some numbers. And give her the scripts for, hmm…Soft Soap, Saddle Soap, Wear-out…. Oh yeah, give her the forms too. Don't forget the forms."

Wasn't I supposed to sign something? The social security number on my inner arm seemed to burn, the ink as cold as neon, even though I didn't particularly want to write it down for anybody. What I wanted was to scratch it off, but secretly, in some locked ladies' room down the hall.

Larry turned back to his desk, pushing more numbers into the phone pad, the cigar glowing.

Louise led me down the row of cubicles.

"Why do they have the curtains?"

She shrugged. "Some people like privacy."

That made sense to me. The curtains weren't much, but at least they'd keep people from looking at you while you talked. People could still probably hear you but at least you didn't have to *see* them hearing you.

I really hated people hearing me when I talked on the phone. It bugged me even if all I was talking about was homework.

Homework. Uh-oh. Brad was probably writing me right this minute.

"Once you get experienced, could you do the calls from home?" I asked.

Louise looked at me as if I was speaking some other language.

"With Wash Your Mouth Out, people kind of call you." She closed her heavy-lidded, heavily-lined, eyes, sighed.

"I mean, if you're doing the soft soap job."

"Don't know nothin' about the soap."

Snapping her gum, she pulled the curtain back from an empty cubicle. "Pigs." She picked up a chips bag and half-filled soda can, then used the bag to wipe the greasy crumbs of chips from the desk onto the floor.

I made a mental note to keep my shoes on.

"So," she said. "You press this green button here to call out, this beige one to redial, and this big red one here to end the call—though you probably won't need that one much."

Then, with a shake of her frosted hair, she started back up the aisle.

"Wait," I whispered urgently. "So, I'm just supposed to sit here and call people?"

But she didn't seem to hear.

XIV.

Soft Soap was terrible. I was terrible. The people I called were terrible.

Wait a second; that's not fair. The people I called weren't exactly terrible; they just didn't like getting calls from me.

Except for one old lady who thought I was her granddaughter and kept asking me how my piano lessons were going. She answered every single question on the form—birth date, place of birth, mother's maiden name, even her social security number, though she was sure, she said, that my mom knew all this stuff already.

Then there was the perv who kept telling me he'd give me his shoe size, but only if I gave him mine first. I told him I didn't need his shoe size, but he couldn't stop talking about it. (13 1/2.)

Most people just hung up.

After about an hour or so, I decided that the only way I would get people to listen to me was if I told them I was giving away a bunch of money. ('Sir, I'm calling from the Unexpected Inheritance Bureau....') I was about to try this, when I heard, just behind me, a deep throaty coo.

It was also kind of a gooey coo. "Oh you are so hot baby, yeah that's right, ooh baby, yeah, give it—"

I pushed the curtain aside. A heavyset woman in a grape-colored track suit and big headset stood just at my back. She had curly brown hair and gold-framed glasses and, in the middle of her next "ooh," gave me a friendly grin.

Then she started to pace the aisle behind me. "Ooh baby—can't you feel it, that soft, firm—"

Suddenly, the business name "Wash Your Mouth Out" took on a whole new meaning. Or, actually, *a* meaning. I hadn't thought about it before. I didn't particularly want to think about it now. I started singing under my breath: *all I want is a room somewhere...far away from the cold night air.*

Only, just then, I would have preferred the cold night air.

"Bye slugger, call me back," said the brown-haired woman into her headset, all the time smiling at me. And now, shifting the mouthpiece, "hi, I'm Selma. You don't mind if I walk up and down back here, do you? Get some exercise?"

(*With one enormous chair*—)

"Oh, hi Selma, I'm, um, Celia."

"Figure this is as good as a treadmill." As her headset buzzed, Selma held up one finger, gave me another grin, and—"howdy big boy, I hoped it'd be you."

She started back up the aisle; I shut the curtain.

It was 7:42. I would do one more call, try to fill out one more form, get paid and get out.

I punched in the next number. The name that lit up was Bessera. Maybe I should have recognized it; I totally didn't.

"Hello," said a male voice.

The script said I should ask if this was the man of the house. I was sick of the script.

"I'm really sorry to bother you, but my name is Celia Pratchett, I go to Spenser High School in New York City, and I wonder if you could, you know, help me."

"You go to Spenser?"

"Yes, and—"

"What class are you in?"

"Um, sophomore."

"What'd you say your name was?"

"Celia, and I'm sorry, but do you mind if I talk to you for a few minutes, and maybe, get your address and stuff?"

"My address?"

"It's for this job I'm doing. I mean, I think they're going to fire me because I'm really bad at it, but I'm supposed to get people's addresses."

The curtain rustled. "Oh baby, talk about hot, you're turning me into an oven, that's right, a red hot soft spunky oven—"

(*Lots of coal making lots of 'eat.*)

I put my hand over the receiver.

"What was that?" the guy at the end of my line asked.

"That's just, look, you don't have to buy anything—"

"What are you selling?"

"Soap."

"I probably won't buy any."

"We've got some for guys."

"Yeah, well...."

"You use soap, don't you?"

"I use it, sure. I just don't buy it."

Did he lift it? (I thought, heart sinking, of Brad.)

"My *mom* buys it," the voice sighed.

"Cool!" I said, too fast.

"Wait a second, are you in Chorus?"

Oh-oh.

(*Warm face, warm 'ands, warm feet—*)

"You're not the pianist?!"

"Yeah. Hey, are you that soprano Ms. Deronda rags on? Celia Pratchett, right? The one with the loud voice."

"It's not really that loud," I whispered.

"No, it's great. Your voice is great."

"Really?!? I mean, it isn't," I said. "But you are. Your playing is terrific."

"Thanks, but what she gives us is pretty straight stuff. What I really play is guitar."

"Seriously? My best friend's dad has a guitar shop in the village."

"Not Get More Guitars."

"Yeah."

"I love that place."

"Look," I said, "I'm sorry, but what's your first name again? I should totally know it, but you know how they are at Spenser—"

"My name is Petry. Petry Bessera."

I found the spot for it on the form.

"And could you tell me your address?"

"Sure."

"Yes," moaned Selma just to my right. "YES...."

"Are you okay?" Petry asked.

"That's ...um, there are a lot of phones here."

"That humongous thing is yours?" Selma crowed.

"Sounds kind of random," Petry said.

I cupped my hand further over the receiver. "So, you like Spenser?" I asked, trying to change the subject.

"I like Chorus."

"Me too. I just wish Ms. Deronda didn't hate me so much."

"She doesn't hate you. She just wants you to blend."

"So I've been told."

"And you do blend most of the time. Sometimes I can really hear you when I play, but most of the time I can only hear you a little.'

"You can hear me? In Chorus?"

"Yeah, you're sort of like the backbone of the whole soprano section. Of the whole Chorus. Your voice is so strong and beautiful."

(*Loverlyyyyy....*)

I didn't know what to say, so looked down at the Soft Soap sheet again. "So, um, how many people are in your household? I mean, do you have brothers and sisters?"

"A little brother—"

"And your parents?"

"Are you trying to fill out your form?"

"Do you mind?"

"Not really."

"It's like a survey. But you don't have to tell me anything personal. You can even, well—you could probably even just make things up. I don't think they're so great here."

"I won't make anything up."

I went through the list of questions. Actually, some of them *were* totally personal. Stuff like whether their family owned their apartment or had a mortgage or wanted a mortgage. How much money his parents made. (That one I was too embarrassed to even ask.)

"That's the hottest, juiciest—" Selma panted; I finally found the mute button.

(*Oh so loverly sitting everlasting blooming...still.*)

Petry told me about himself too. It sounded like he played guitar really well. He even wrote songs. He was in a band, and every once in a while they played a gig. "But not so much," he sighed.

"Why not?"

"We're all busy with school and stuff, and then, my guitar, my electric, is kind of a bummer. It was good when I was younger, but for gigs, it kind of sucks—"

"You can't get a new one?"

"My dad wants me to concentrate on the piano. That's one reason I was glad to be the accompanist for Chorus. He loves that." He sighed. "Besides, good guitars are expensive."

"Can you earn anything with your band?"

"A little," he laughed. "And I walk dogs."

"You walk dogs?" I pictured Petry at the Chorus piano with a bunch of leashes tangling around the bench, Ms. Deronda growing fangs.

"You know the Village. There are tons of them. I like dogs and it pays pretty well."

"Cool."

"You ready?" he said, voice quieter. "Got everything?"

"Huh?"

"Sorry, Celia. Gotta go. You need anything else for your form?"

"No, um, thanks. Thanks a lot."

"Yeah, I'm set." He spoke into the distance again.

"Ooh baby," Selma moaned (not in the distance).

(*All I want is a room....*)

"Give it—" Selma went on.

"Bye," I said.

XV.

"I got two," I told Larry as I handed over my forms.

"In three and a half hours? You're an ace."

You were the one that promised $1200 an hour, I fumed inside. "Sorry," I said.

He shook his head, the cigar hanging from his mouth like a fat brown (smoldering) toothpick.

"People don't like to get called by strangers," I tried.

"You're supposed to act like their friend."

I took a deep breath. "So, two is like thirty dollars, right? "

"Hey, these are pretty good." He scanned one of my pages slowly. "Yeah, these we can sell to all sorts of folks."

"Sell?"

"We got folks pay good money for stuff like this."

"But that's like identity theft!"

"Hold on there, kid." He waved the pieces of paper at me. "We don't steal nothin' from nobody."

"But that old lady, Mrs. Sloop, thought I was her granddaughter, and Petry goes to my school."

"Now, there's an idea. They got a directory at your school?"

That did it. I grabbed the two forms out of his smudged hands. I moved so fast that the only thing that tried to stop me was the cigar, which, because it wasn't actually attached to him, dropped right onto his beach ball belly.

"Holy Bejesus!" he cried, batting sparks from his gut.

Forms in fist, I dashed into the hallway.

"Yo, Nosey, you come back here!"

I slammed the elevator's down button, then, remembering how glacially slow it was, lunged into the dingy stairwell. The air (the little there was) was thick with old cigarette. Holding my breath, I scampered down the stairs until I got to a door that said LOBBY in scratched-out black letters, then pushed. It didn't budge, didn't budge, didn't BUDGE, till—*whammo!*—I was propelled onto something hard and flat.

"Jesus Maria!"

I sprawled over the security guard's desk. He had flung himself against the wall, and now was pulling out his nightstick.

But I was already out the door, running as fast as I could across the street, rapping hard on the hood of one cab that swerved towards me, then down the opposite sidewalk until, heart pounding, I'd gone at least ten blocks.

Now that I was far enough away for a measure of safety, I carefully tore each crumpled form into bits and deposited the little flakes into the next six blocks of trash receptacles—five times darting across the street, three times even lifting the lids off dumpsters, shutting my eyes so that if a rat jumped out, I didn't have to see it. (Actually, *half*-shutting my eyes, so that if a rat jumped out, I could scream and get out of the way.)

I worked like a shredding machine on wheels, making sure that no one would ever be able to piece together the personal information of either Petry Bessera or Mrs. Amelia Sloop.

I slipped the final flakes of form through the slit of a partly-opened dumpster in the meat-packing district, just below 14th Street. This was totally heroic on my part. (If a rat jumped out of one of the big meat-packing dumpsters, it would be a super-vicious meat-stuffed rat.)

"Where were you?" my mom asked when I slumped into our apartment. "I called you five times!"

"Job hunting."

After a closer look, her face turned sympathetic. "No luck, huh?"

"The guy I was supposed to work for called me 'Nosey.'" Tears seeped into my voice. Idiotic tears.

"Sounds like you wouldn't want that job anyway," my mom said.

XVI.

The name "Nosey" echoed in my head all the next morning. The only thing that made me feel better was seeing Petry. That was kind of magical. He was at the school entrance when I walked in, standing by the security guards.

"I'm sorry, I don't know where it is," he said, feeling his pockets.

"Can't let you in without an ID," the guard said.

"Can I sign for him?" I asked.

Petry smiled at me, a sweet asymmetrical toothy smile. "Hey," he said.

Okay, so he didn't have the most perfect teeth, and maybe 'hey' wasn't the absolutely coolest thing he could have said.

(Though, actually, I thought it was one of them.)

I smiled back brightly. (Too brightly. Did I want to come off as a light bulb?)

"Got to go to the office," the guard said.

"But you *know* me," Petry said, turning back to him. "I go through here three or four times a day."

"Ain't got an ID, got to go to the office."

I walked with Petry across the hall.

"I'm late too," he grimaced.

"You have first period?"

"Yeah."

"Maybe you should have tried downstairs. She's nicer."

"If I'd known I didn't have my ID—"

It was a lot harder to talk to Petry in person than on the phone. There was his hair for one thing, not sun-bleached or styled, but clean and fresh, and full of, you know, locks. He shook some out of his face. "So how was the rest of the job?"

"Terrible," I groaned. "They didn't even pay me."

"Employers, man, they can be the pits."

"Yeah."

"You really need the extra dough though, huh?"

"Totally."

"Me too. Hah. You know all about my needing money." He laughed and shook his hair out of eyes again. Was there a twinkle in them? My heart swelled, even if there wasn't.

"You know, you were pretty good at that job, making people talk. They *should* have paid you," he said.

I shrugged, playing it cool. We were in front of the office now.

"I wanted to tell you—I heard about a gig last night," he went on. "It doesn't look so great, but it would be—"

"But I'm not in a band—"

"It's not a music gig," he smiled. "Just a job."

"Really?"

"Sure. Hey, give me a call. You got my number, right?" He laughed again. Now there was a definite twinkle.

I laughed too. Until he disappeared into the office, and I realized that I'd thrown his number away the night before with my fistfuls of torn paper.

I walked slowly into Bio. We spent the whole period watching a movie about melting ice floes. Apparently, we were taking a break from cell structure and ATP. (Maybe because Ms. Bryan also taught Environmental Science.)

As doomed baby polar bears tumbled across the screen, I hoped Maddy and her boyfriend could do something.

As fetching as baby polar bears were, I soon found myself thinking about Petry.

I wished I could hear him play the guitar. I wished *I* could play the guitar.

Hey, maybe Petry could teach me. If I could learn to play, we could maybe play and sing together—

My mind—my crazed, musical-filled mind—jumped to Julie Andrews again, only now she had a guitar in her lap, and was surrounded by mountains and little Von Trapps. It was the beginning of the whole *Doe a Deer* sequence.

I tried to squelch the gush of song inside.

(*A female deer.*)

But it was too late.

(*Ray, a drop of golden sun.*)

My face burned in the darkness of the Bio lab. I don't know why I felt so embarrassed. It wasn't as if anyone could hear me. (The most that they might notice was a curious swaying of my torso. It sometimes does that when I sing inside.)

But it wasn't the danger of unconscious swaying that bothered me. It was the fact that it was so hard to imagine Petry as a *Sound of Music* fan. I mean, he wore all those rocker t-shirts, right? He'd probably think I was a total idiot.

I didn't even think Brad was very *Sound-of-Music* sympathetic, and he might be planning to direct it.

I willed my brain to stop singing.

(*Me, a name I call myself.*)

But couldn't.

(*Far, a long long way to run.*)

If only the musical wasn't going to be televised, if only Brad liked me, if only I could get Hank fixed in time—

(*Sew, a needle pulling thread—*)

After Bio, I met Deanna at her locker, where she was checking out her highlights (hot pink that day).

She looked terrible. Not just the hot pink hair—she was all hot pink, actually—she looked upset, eyes puffy, cheeks stained.

"You okay?" I asked.

She turned from her locker mirror. "My dad got robbed last night."

"Oh Dee! They didn't hurt him?!"

"Only broke his heart."

"No! Is he in the hospital?"

"Huh? No, it was the store that was robbed, not my dad. Not personally. It was Get More Guitars. Someone broke in and stole his favorite guitar. He'd only had it for like five minutes, but he'd wanted it for ages. It used to be Eric Clapton's."

"Eric Clapton--wasn't he the guy from that band you were telling me about. Cream?"

"Yeah. The store was holding it for him. Eric Clapton's like his idol. It was a super valuable guitar."

"I'm so sorry."

"He was going to let me play it too."

"You know how to play the guitar?"

"I was going to learn," Deanna said, turning sullen. "That was the whole point. But now some stupid jerk has ripped it off. A kid from here too. Can you believe it? They found a Spenser ID. Right on the scene. Must have been one dumb kid."

"A kid from Spenser? Seriously?"

She turned back to her locker mirror, rearranging the hot pink strands of her bangs. "'My dad won't tell me who until the police make the arrest. All I can say is that he better not have sold it."

I felt genuinely sympathetic towards Deanna, her dad too, even though the whole story seemed kind of weird. Deanna had never been what I called musical, except maybe in the listening area. Her life had also never been exactly short on guitars. I mean, if she had wanted to learn to play, she could have learned a long time ago.

And the idea that a kid from Spenser would break in to her dad's store to steal something—

That seemed bizarre too. Even though Spenser was a pretty big school. All kinds of things probably happened here that I didn't know about.

"Uh oh." I looked up at a hall clock that I knew from experience was exactly five hours and ten minutes late. "Dee, come on!"

XVII.

Second bell had already rung, but still we sprinted across the bright planking of the gym, running faster than we ever did in gym class itself.

"Oh, crap," Deanna said, trying to turn the locker room handle.

It was locked, and Ms. Pavlova was probably already back in her office, counting down the seconds until she could take off more grade points.

"We're going to end up in summer school gym," Deanna wailed. "You know that, don't you?"

I knew that; I remembered something else too: kids failing a class at Spenser were banned from extracurricular activities for the duration of the term, even if the extracurricular was the school musical and the kid's brain was haunted by musicals. If you were failing, even just in first marking period, you were out.

I scanned the empty gym. "No, come on, let's try...." There were bleachers, basketball hoops, big wooden cabinets for balls, a couple of large trash cans.

"Here!" I began to run again, pulling—dragging—Deanna to the far corner of the gym next to one of the large trash cans. "You've got your gym clothes, right? Change back there."

"Behind the trash can? Eeuuw."

"Come on, Dee. You go first, I'll stand guard."

"I can't even fit back there."

I edged the trash can from the wall, willing the metal not to squeal as I dragged it over the polyurethane.

"Don't touch it," Deanna warned (as if I hadn't already).

I rubbed my hands on my jeans. "It's just a trash can." (Yuck.) "Hurry."

"I'm keeping on my tights. I don't care if I get runs."

"Fine."

Even though she kept her tights on, Deanna took forever. At last, she squeezed out from behind the can. I jumped into her place.

In the middle of taking off my jeans—I wasn't wearing tights—I looked over to see Deanna sitting down on the floor, messing with her sneaker laces. "Dee! You're supposed to be guarding me!"

Just at that moment (of course), Pradip Singh and Prem Chowdry stepped out from the boys locker room, their eyes widening at the sight of my bare behind. Okay, I had on bikini underwear—

"Get out!" Deanna shrieked.

Pradip and Prem scurried back into the locker room.

Her shriek, well-honed by little brothers, was one of the things I'd always admired about Deanna.

"Where are we going to put our stuff?" she hissed.

"Back here?" I pointed to the narrow space behind the trash can.

"Won't she see?"

"How about—*in* the trash can?" I pushed open the flap for garbage. "We can put them just on the top, then get them out next period."

"Celia," she said, in a tone that meant 'no way.' "I have an English paper in this pack."

"Then how about...um...how about that place they keep the basketballs? You know, under the bleachers?"

"She won't see?"

"Aren't we just doing stupid exercises?"

Ms. Pavlova had been torturing us with calisthenics for the last couple of weeks.

"Oh, yeah."

We scrambled over to the big wooden bin where the balls were kept. Other kids were slouching out of the locker rooms now, Pradip and Prem in the rear.

"Hurry," Deanna whispered. I lifted the wooden top, ready to stuff our packs down, but the bin was crammed with basketballs. There was simply no space.

"Take some out."

We each took two balls out, stuck our backpacks in, gently gently placed the balls onto the floor.

Just in time. As we hurried to our places in the line, Ms. Pavlova stepped from her office, leafing through her attendance book.

"Allcott."

"Present."

"Bardowsky."

"Present."

"Bremer."

"Present."

'Chan, Linda."

"Present."

"Chan, Kevin."

"Present."

A boy swung through the door to the gym. Ms. Pavlova looked up to him. "I hope you have no plans for summer, Leder."

Although Deanna and I did not stand next to each other, I could feel her eyes straining to where the basketballs had started to crawl. They gathered together like guilty puppies who have just left incriminating evidence on the rug.

I could feel Pradip and Prem's eyes too. Actually, I could *see* their eyes. They alternated between looking at me, Deanna, and the four wayward balls.

(*When you're a jet, you're a jet all the way—*)

That is a totally great song from *West Side Story*. The gang members sing it right at the beginning of the musical, keeping the beat with snapping fingers and a refrain of *cool, man, real cool*.

I wasn't quite sure why it had popped in my head. Certainly not because I felt cool.

I became conscious, then, of another pair of eyes.

Petry Bessera. I'd almost forgotten he was in my gym class. How could I have almost forgotten that?

He was looking at me with a soft half-smile.

"Who brought balls out?" Ms. Pavlova asked, her Russian accent dialed to the accusatory. "Will who took out put back, please?"

No one spoke. Ms. Pavlova compressed her thin pre-tightened lips.

"Will person playing with balls step please forward and put back, so class can begin?"

The class stared down at its collective sneakers.

(*You're never alone. You're never disconnected.*)

That was the lilty fast part of the song. I tried to keep my feet from breaking into a nervous dance step.

"Szo," Ms. Pavlova said, emphasizing the "z." "We will stand. Chan, Kevin—do you hear?"

Kevin Chan must have been doing something suspicious. *Something* anyway. (Anything was suspicious to Ms. Pavlova.)

"Until person who took out balls step forward. One...two... three...."

I thought of how I'd crumpled the forms in the face of that guy, Larry, the night before. I thought of Maddy too. She would have organized a school-wide petition by this point. Down with Pavlova! Unfair treatment to Fourth Period Gym!

(*You're home with your own.*

When company's expected

you're well pro——-tected.)

And then, in the midst of an internal finger-snap, my gaze drifted over to Ms. Pavlova's face. It looked grey, nervous, unhappy.

Deanna always said Ms. Pavlova was trying to get people into summer gym just so she herself could have a summer job. That story suddenly made me feel sorry for her. My limited work experience had already given me a sense of how hard it was to earn extra money— any money. Maybe Ms. Pavlova had a child to support, or a mother, or grandmother. I pictured an old Russian lady I'd seen in a *National Geographic* (crinkled scarf, crinkled eyes, crinkled cheeks) and was about to step forward and pick up the stupid balls, when—

"I'll get 'em, Ms. Pavlova," Petry said.

"You took out?"

"No, ma'am. I think they were taken out by some kids between classes."

As Petry loped across the gym, I remembered why we'd had to take the balls out of the bin to begin with.

"Oh no! My foot!' I cried, collapsing onto the floor. "I've got this cramp or splinter or—"

I usually think of myself as a singer rather than an actress. But I must act pretty well because Ms. Pavlova's usual nastiness was instantly replaced by concern.

"Pull toes back, forward, back again," she said, leaning over me.

"Oh," I moaned.

"You stand up?"

"I'm not sure."

The rest of the class grouped strategically around us. I slowly got to my feet as Petry, who must have been both (a) strong, and (b) good at geometry, stepped back into the group, aiming one of his slightly goofy, toothy, non-surfer smiles at me.

"It's getting better," I blushed.

"You go to school nurse?"

"No, it's…fine. It was just a…foot cramp."

"Aha. The cramp," Ms. Pavlova sighed. "I used to get them in performance, oh so terrible; sometimes right foot, sometimes left."

"You did performance?"

Ms. Pavlova shrugged dismissively. "Provincial troupes. And mostly, how you say, the corps."

My brain filled with apples until I focused on Ms. Pavlova's turned-out feet and the careful bun of hair at the back of her head.

"Ballet?"

"But now the calisthenics, yes? Conditioning, yes? You there, Williams; Lee, Tiffany."

Ms. Pavlova re-centered herself. "Back to barre," she barked. "You two," she pointed at Prem and Pradip. "You, Bessera—thanks for help with balls. Now push-up, class. What did I say? Push *Up*! And a one, and a two—"

I hunkered down into something like a push-up position.

(*Cool, man, real cool.*)

XVIII.

If it was strange thinking of Ms. Pavlova as a ballet master, it was even stranger to think of Petry as the guy who saved Deanna and me, for the moment anyway, from summer school gym.

No, not just the guy who saved us from summer school gym, our friend.

Actually, strange wasn't the right word. Try *great.*

After Ms. Pavlova went back to her office at the end of the class, he helped me and Deanna extract our stuff from the bin, then smiled: "you want me to stand guard?"

I wondered whether Hank, when bright red, looked particularly beet-like, and whether Petry would think it strange if I put my hand over it. I made myself shrug instead, arms to my sides. "We were late."

He said something about Ms. Pavlova; I said something about Ms. Pavlova; he, looking across the gym, said something about the whole thing being a pain; I, looking at my feet, said something about the whole thing being a pain, and then "Hey Ceel—" Deanna called from the gym doorway. "See you later."

"Oh geez—I've got to get up to the tenth floor," I said, running after her.

"Good luck," Petry called.

I sprinted up the stairs.

When I'd been talking to Petry, his face had been kind of a blur, but now that I was running up the stairs, I seemed to see it again, I mean, *really* see it.

It was a sweet face. Okay, his teeth weren't perfect. He was awfully pale. His nose was kind of hawkish too, but in a way that looked good on a boy, *and* he had this cool musician thing going on—

BRRRRRIIINNNNGGG!!!!!!

Damn.

I was late and I had Pre-Cal and I'd have to wear my gym shorts, stupid gym shorts that didn't even say 'pink' on the behind, into a room where I was going to have to sit right next to Brad, who might not have much of a musician thing going on, but did have the word 'beautiful' stamped indelibly on every part of his body—

As I sped through the hallway, I tried to get back into the "Jet" song, but couldn't. Was there a dork song?

Slipping into the classroom, I held my backpack over my thighs. *I feel pretty,* also from *West Side Story,* suddenly began circulating around my mortified brain. Maybe it was lodged in the next set of neurons.

(*Oh so pretty.*)

I tried to tell myself that a lot of kids wore shorts when it was warm out.

The girls' soccer team wore shorts during last period even when it was freezing. It was either that or change on the subway.

(*And I pity any girl who isn't me today.*)

Nobody pitied the legs of the girls' soccer team. They were legs that slide-tackled, legs that kicked.

My legs were not particularly strong, and, just at this moment, were speckled with goose pimples. The only thing they had going for them was that they were regularly shaved.

(*I feel charming, oh so charming,*

It's alarming how charming I feel.)

Oh yeah. The *West Side Story* of my brain might have felt charming, but the east, north, and south side stories felt about as alluring as Shrek.

But you know what? After a minute or so of mind-numbing embarrassment, I realized that my Shrek legs didn't matter. Brad totally didn't register them. He was too busy bending over the teeny nose and huge chest of this girl, Trina Manning, who had the seat right behind mine.

"So," Brad said, leaning into Trina's scoop-necked t-shirt, "I'm planning on a pre-pre-audition meeting. But it's going to be kind of private. Just the student director—that's me, right?—and the people who will probably end up getting cast in the final show."

He smiled meaningfully into Trina's cleavage. "You up for it?"

Trina smiled back, her lip gloss reflecting Brad's perfect bone structure.

(*See that pretty girl in the mirror there,*

Who can that attractive girl be?)

Come on, Celia. Why shouldn't Trina be in the show? She was a senior; it would be her last chance to do theater at Spenser.

Sure, my brain replied. Except that Trina had never cared one bit about theater. She was a cheerleader—a *cheerleader*.

Hey, Brad I'm here, I wanted to shout, the girl who does *all* your Pre-Cal homework.

Instead of shouting, I kicked my chair. I hoped for a soft but decisive clink, but, unfortunately, my foot got tangled in the metal rod that connected the chair to the desk and we all three (me, desk, chair) lurched noisily across the floor.

It got Brad's attention. Everyone else's too.

Brad, at least, smiled,

(*Such a pretty smile!*)

I felt my anger melting, every bit of it.

Well, almost every bit. When, even as Brad smiled at me, he also squeezed Trina's shoulder, some of that anger firmed right back up. Until, after the squeeze, he flashed the glow back on me again.

(*Such a pretty meeeee!*)

"A lot of homework last night, huh?" he sighed, stepping to his seat.

"Totally," I said. (*'Totally!?'*)

But Brad just smiled at me again, a smile that was so beautiful it almost seemed sweet. Maybe, I thought desperately, he'd invite me to this pre-pre-audition meeting too, if I just explained how important it was to me.

"You know, Brad," I said with forced casualness. "I don't just do math. I sing, too. I'm in Chorus."

"Oh yeah?" He flipped through his notebook.

"I'm a soprano," I fake-laughed. "One of the loudest ones."

(Lame. Lame, lame, lame.)

"Cool," he said, opening his math book.

"Yeah." My face flushed. "Ms. Deronda, you know, the Chorus director—she's always ragging on me because my voice is so, um, loud. It's like I'm always singing a solo or something, like some singer in a Broadway musical. You know, like Barbra Streisand."

(Celia, no! Not Barbra Streisand! The point was to *divert* attention from the schnoz!!!!)

Brad stared down at his book. Just now he had to focus on Pre-Cal?

"Man, I hate math," he said. "You mind if I talk to you about it tonight."

I knew that by "talk" he meant chat online and by "about it" he meant get the answers.

What could I say? 'Yes, if you'll invite me to the pre-pre-audition meeting.' 'Yes, if you'll at least *consider* giving me a part.' 'Yes, if you'll even just listen to me sing for a minute.'

I really didn't want to trade Pre-Cal homework for a part. But how else was I going to get one?

(*I feel stunning*

And entrancing—)

Not.

"Cool," I whispered back.

There had to be another way. But what? How could I get a nose job without a nose job job?

My eyes stung, my throat lumped.

Stop right there, Celia. What had Petry said this morning? That he knew about some gig.

I'd see him next period too, in A.P. Spanish.

(*Feel like running*

91

And dancing for joy—)

Wait a second, the cautious part of my brain warned. You don't even know what the gig is yet.

But the other part of my brain (the main part) didn't care.

IXX.

I sped out of my gym clothes after Pre-Cal—I couldn't take another hour as Shrek—but still got to A.P. Spanish too late to talk to Petry before class.

We had assigned seating there too. Petry had gotten himself assigned to the back. As I walked past him, I saw that he had a folder open inside his notebook filled with what looked like sheet music.

He noticed me and smiled his not perfect but genuinely enthusiastic, though not dorkily enthusiastic, smile.

I felt my cheeks heating up again. Celia, since when were you part Bunsen burner? I asked myself, but, to tell the truth, the heat made me feel kind of wonderful.

Until the two policemen showed up.

They came right to the door of the classroom, waiting, while Principal Eggars, who was with them, cleared his throat. Then all three of them huddled by Señora Gomez's desk.

"Petry," she said after a moment. "Can you come, please."

In Spanish, Señora Gomez's voice was low, sultry, confident; but she spoke English now and her words wobbled, high-pitched and insecure.

Petry looked up from his music, face confused.

"Better bring your things," Principal Eggars said.

The cops watched Petry gather his stuff; we all did.

The bottom of my stomach hovered someplace in my throat. Maybe it was from hanging out with Maddy—the sight of expectant policemen put me on a serious edge.

I wanted to tell Petry to run, only it flashed through my mind as "¡corre!" It seemed that if I could just shout out in Spanish, Petry could sprout a black cape and leap, Zorro-like, over the cops.

But I didn't shout "¡corre!" and Petry, looking even paler than normal, folded up his books, put them in an army surplus shoulder bag that bore a Jimi Hendrix badge, and walked to the front of the classroom.

One of the policeman nodded, "Are you Peter—Petey... Bess—Besser?"

Petry nodded.

"Come along son," said the other cop, and, one on each side of Petry, they left the classroom, Principal Eggars just behind.

All eyes followed them out the door. Bijou Larkin, who was just about the biggest gossip in the whole school, scurried over to watch them walk down the hall. Other people stood to join her, till Señora Gomez, walking to the door herself, said (now in her firm Spanish voice), "Sientese—Bijou! Seintese."

Then she too stared down the hall.

I felt sick.

By the time Spanish ended, the hall was buzzing.

"Hey, what was that?"

"Does he sell dope, man?"

"You'd know that already, dude."

"Get to class, people," the government teacher, Mr. Russo, ordered from the doorway of his room. "Or I'm writing out detention slips for every single one of you."

As the jumble dissolved—"you there, Brinkman! You there, Mesri!"—I saw Deanna. She was walking slowly but talking a mile a minute to two other sophomores, Cindy Carlyle and Rick Janawicz.

I caught up with them.

"I just hope you get your guitar back," Rick said.

"Me too. And now that they've caught the guy," Cindy nodded, "sounds like you will."

"What guy?" I asked.

"That kid in gym," Deanna said. Then, "bye guys," giving Cindy and Rick a quick wave.

Mr. Russo was walking toward us, eyes like bullets. Deanna and I automatically adjusted our speed to 'scoot' till we turned a convenient corner.

"What kid in gym?"

"You know, that kid Bessera. It was his ID at my dad's store. That's why the police came. Did you see them?"

"Petry Bessera?"

"Yeah, that's him. The kid with the basketballs. Crazy, right? That it would be him?"

"But, Deanna, it just couldn't have been Petry who broke into your dad's store. It just couldn't have been."

"Celia," Deanna said, forcing a dose of patience into her voice. "It was great he helped us in gym and all, but it was his ID."

"I don't care whose ID it was. It wasn't him."

"And why not? Because he's capable of *not* being a thief every once in a while? You don't even know the guy."

I was ready to burst out about Soft Soap, how I'd talked to Petry on the phone, and then how I'd talked to him this morning by the door, this morning when he hadn't...had his ID....

"Look, he plays piano for Chorus," I fumbled.

"So?"

"Somebody who plays the piano like he does wouldn't steal a guitar."

"Maybe pianos are just too heavy to sneak."

"Dee—," I started, but she was already walking away, a great big 'so there' in the swing of her hips.

I tried to put a little 'so there' into my step too, but I felt too low for much swing.

How could Petry have been arrested?

This wasn't like one of Maddy's arrests. They were for minor stuff, like being in an unlicensed protest march, or handing out leaflets too close to a voting booth.

This was for stealing, theft, maybe even *grand larceny*.

And, of course, Deanna was upset. Her dad had been robbed of something important to him; it seemed to be important to her too.

But Petry couldn't have been the thief; he just couldn't have been. Not with that kind goofy smile.

And then I thought of Brad again, Brad with the smile so beautiful that it almost seemed sweet.

And then I felt lower than ever.

XX.

I thought Deanna might be too mad to meet me after school, but there she was, hanging against the brickwork just outside the double doors, some of the duct tape from her purse and backpack actually sticking to the brickwork—

I didn't say hello; she didn't either.

"Is it completely impossible to get any decent food around this place?" she grumbled.

We hiked over to the Cheese Wheel without another word.

Normally, I didn't pay much attention to all the special deals coating the store's glass windows, since Deanna got us everything we wanted for free. (I usually tried to make it up to her by buying us cappuccinos at Rocco's down the block.) Today, though, there was something on the glass that caught my eye: a "part-time help needed" sign.

A job! A part-time job! A job that I might actually be able to get because I knew the people hiring!

Who were kind of mad at me at the moment.

And whose favors I hated to ask anyway. I mean, Deanna was my best friend, not my networking contact.

As I wondered how, and whether, I could bring any of this up, she chatted with Marcel.

"Bonjour Bossgirl," he smirked.

"Bonjour Marcel," Deanna said, her eyes studying the wedges and rounds of cheese in the glass case below him.

Although Deanna's dad owned the Cheese Wheel, it was Marcel who ran the place. He was a tall French guy who always wore a dark beret from which tendrils of hennaed hair peeked out. A little precious; but hey, he was French. And the guy totally knew cheese.

Deanna ordered our favorite snack—a wedge of Brie and a baguette—in clipped tones. Then she pulled out her cell, checked her texts, and after breaking off a big hunk of baguette for herself, handed me the bag.

"My dad's down the block," she said, meaning Get More Guitars. (Although Mr. Zenia owned the guitar store, he didn't hang there much. I guessed he was only there now because of the theft.)

"I need to talk to him, okay?" she went on. "You mind waiting?"

"No problem. Unless maybe I should go on home?"

"Nah, just, you know, sit back by the cookbooks."

Okay, so she was still mad. (Normally we went everywhere together.)

But not totally mad. (She didn't tell me to just go home.)

A part of me felt miffed not to go with her to see her dad. It would be my chance to tell Mr. Zenia that Petry was innocent, that the police were making a big mistake.

Which would be terrific, *if* I had a way to prove the police were making a big mistake. All I had was my absolute certainty that a guy who played the piano so well, who wouldn't even lie on a phone survey, who had such a sweet *toothy* smile, would not steal a guitar, especially not Eric Clapton's guitar.

Better to wait until I could come up with something a little more concrete, I thought. Better not to lose my credibility. (That was one of Maddy's watchwords.)

At least the Cheese Wheel was a cool place to hang. The smell of all that cheese always made me feel as if I were in Europe somewhere, at least like I imagined Europe to be. The staff didn't mind if you sat down in the books and magazines section. That was in the back of the store, behind the small assortment of cookware. The magazines were comfy, and, back there, you could hardly hear the bell tones that rang each time the door opened, much less Marcel and Zach's softly accented voices. (Zach was the other guy who worked there. From Morocco, he was also a native French speaker.)

As I tore at the neck of the baguette, trying to direct the shower of flakes into the paper bag that still held the cheese, I thought about *bread*. What was the French word for it? I took Spanish now, but I'd had a year of French back in middle school.

Pan? No.

Pain? Yes, that was it. I wasn't sure of the pronunciation, but remembered that it was spelled like that. P-a-i-n. I remembered because that had been a big joke in our class: that French spelling was a *pain* in the *derriere*. (In language class, just about anything passes for a joke.)

But now, sitting on those glossy food magazines, the whole thing seemed exactly right to me. Bread. What a pain. Petry needing it for a new guitar. Me needing it for a new nose.

Wait a sec. Should I just go talk to Marcel myself? Ask *him* about the job advertised in the window?

A big part of me wanted to jump up and race to the counter.

But a bigger part—my *derriere*—stayed glued to the cooking magazines. First, because…well, it's not so easy to jump up and ask someone for a job.

Secondly, because it seemed weird to ask for a job at Deanna's father's store without even mentioning it to her.

Even though it felt almost as weird to mention it to her.

If only life were like a Broadway musical.

I could picture the scene: the clock up above me would start to tick loudly; my head, as I looked through a book on *Fondue And Other Swiss Favorites,* would start to bob back and forth in time with it. My shoe would start tapping too after a second, also in time with the clock, and pretty soon, I'd begin singing something like Eliza in *My Fair Lady,* when she finally learns to say the A's in rain and Spain and plain.

(*Bed! Bed! I couldn't go to bed! My head's too light to try to set it down!*)

Except in my Cheese Wheel song, the line would be something like, "*Cheese! Cheese! I haven't had an ounce. Still I find it putting on the pounds!*"

Or maybe not.

Because if I were in a Broadway musical, the song would just about have to end with me polkaing around the aisles with Marcel, who, through the refrain, would outfit me with a chef's hat and apron, and Deanna, who would hand me a big bite of skewered Swiss.

Oops. Here she was, Swiss cheese not in hand. I stood up quickly, spraying flakes of crust onto the floor, then tried to silently scrape them under the magazine rack with my feet.

Deanna didn't notice. She tore off another piece of baguette, showering the floor with even more flakes.

(*'Crumbs! Crumbs!'* my brain sang, *'we're making all these crumbs!'*)

"It *was* your darling Petry, by the way," Deanna sniffed. "Not only did they find his ID, they got him on tape."

"What?"

"Security video. It may be a hard sell in court, my dad says. It's mainly his back. But you know that goony t-shirt he wears."

"Cream?" I moaned.

She nodded. "That's another bit of evidence too—looks like the guy's obsessed with Clapton. The shot also shows his hair."

"No!" I said, feeling sick.

"Yep. And they've got the time he was there: 7:53. The Cheese Wheel was open till 8, but Get More Guitars was already closed. Your Petry must be really good at picking locks by the way. Maybe it helps to play the piano."

"He's not *my* Petry."

"He just better give my guitar back."

It amazed me how, in the course of a couple of conversations, it had gone from being Eric Clapton's guitar to Deanna's dad's guitar to Deanna's guitar. Deanna, who didn't even play guitar. But I didn't mention that.

Because she was normally my friend.

I mean, she *was* my friend.

"Wait a second. 7:53?"

"Yeah, it's time-stamped."

"But Petry couldn't have been in the guitar store at 7:53."

"Celia, they've got it on tape."

"Yes, but I called him at around 7:42. On his home phone. We talked for a long time."

"You called Bessera? I thought you didn't even know the guy."

I told her about Soft Soap. (Well, I skipped the phone sex part. And Larry's calling me "Nosey.") But I went through everything else—how I had to fill out forms, how I'd somehow happened to call Petry, how I'd torn up all the forms afterwards. As Deanna listened, she poked through the bag, taking thoughtful fingerfuls of creamy cheese and chalk-white cheese rind. (Yes, it was gross, but we'd already eaten all the baguette.)

"Celia," she said, after I finished. "I know you like this guy. Even I like the guy. But they caught him on tape. On *tape*."

I wanted to say, "they caught his back."

I wanted to say, "didn't your dad have that guitar insured?"

I wanted to say, "how can you believe everything people tell you?"

If only it were all one big Broadway musical, we could all just dance and sing and laugh about the whole thing.

Or maybe this would be the drama section of the play, where the outraged townspeople, all of whom looked like variations of Deanna (even the guys with the sideburns and mustaches), would stand staunchly center-stage, fingers pointing accusingly at the play's hero.

Wait a second. If this were a musical, who would the hero *be*? Petry? Brad?

And what about, um, *me*?

XXI.

All the rest of the evening I thought about Petry.

And the job.

And Hank.

And Brad.

And the musical.

And Hank.

And Petry again.

I wondered how to reach him without his cell or email. I tried to "friend" him on Facebook, even though that felt incredibly embarrassing somehow. But his page was blocked. (Had he blocked it himself? The police? His parents?)

I wasn't sure what I was going to say even if I *did* reach him. "I'm sorry you got arrested," seemed kind of inadequate.

Then I realized (duh!) that I was his alibi. Of course, I'd have something to say to him.

I finally did a white pages search. Several numbers came up, but I remembered that when I wrote Petry's address down for Soft Soap, it had been in the Village.

"Hello" said an adult male voice. Petry's dad?

"Is this, um, the residence of Petry Bessera?"

"Who's calling, please?"

"Could I speak to him?"

"I'm sorry, miss. Petry's not taking calls right now."

My heart stopped. "He's not in jail?"

"What did you say your name was?"

"I'm sorry. I'm Celia, Celia Pratchett… and I, well…" I thought suddenly about how my mom felt when Maddy was arrested. "You know Petry didn't do it?"

"What do you mean?"

"I mean, you *know* he didn't steal the guitar, right? I was talking to him on this number—this is your home number, right?—from 7:42 until like 8, so I can totally testify."

"And you are *whom*, precisely? One of Petry's girlfriends?"

(Petry had *girlfriends*?)

"I'm just a friend," I said, flushing. "What I'm trying to say is that I was talking to Petry right around the time the guitar was supposedly stolen, right here on his home phone. Which means he just couldn't have stolen it."

"That's very loyal of you, young lady. But did it ever occur to you that people can forward their phone calls to another phone, for example, a cell phone?"

"He—really?"

"It's been known to happen. So please, though we appreciate your wish to help Petry, it would be better if you called some other time."

"Like later?"

"*Like*," the man said sternly, "after Petry returns the guitar."

Click.

I pulled the phone from my ear. When Maddy got into trouble, we knew she'd probably done at least some of what the police said. Still, my mom was on her side. "I know this child and she does *not* resist arrest," she always insisted.

Petry's dad seemed ready to send Petry to prison himself.

And what was that about forwarding my Soft Soap call? The line had been so clear.

Well, maybe not *so* clear.

But Petry was totally calm. He wasn't even breathing heavily.

(But with Selma panting behind you, would you have noticed?)

I *would* have noticed a lock being picked, a steel gate going up.

Wouldn't I?

Except that maybe I talked to him after the lock had already been picked, after the steel gate was already up—it was his back, Deanna said.

I thought of Brad's hand in the refrigerator case. I thought of how he had stolen a beer while I just stood there, doing nothing.

Feeling totally rank, I sat down in front of my computer. The minute I signed on, two orange lights blinked at the bottom of the screen.

Boymeetsgirl17: You got the math?

I tried to get excited by the fact that Brad was becoming seriously dependent on me.

Bluesong: Not yet.

Pinkwstripes: Hey.

Deanna was on too.

Bluesong: Hey.

Pinkwstripes: Sorry I upset u.

Bluesong: It's ok.

Pinkwstripes: There's a part-time job at the Cheese Wheel. U see?

Bluesong: Saw.

Pinkwstripes: My dad said u could have it, if u want. Cuz he knows u.

Bluesong: Really!!!?

Boymeetsgirl17: Is it soup yet?

I tried not to think about how goony that would have sounded if *I* had written it.

Bluesong: Not yet.

Pinkwstripes: He'll talk to Marcel.

Bluesong: Thank him so much!!!

Pinkwstripes: I think it's only weekends.

My heart fell. Not *fell*. My heart, which had been jumping, sat down. If the job was only on weekends, it would be impossible to earn enough to get my nose done over Christmas.

On the other hand, I might just be able to earn enough to get it done during spring break. That would be after auditions, but probably before the actual show.

Not perfect. But, if I kept doing Brad's homework—

I got out my math.

XXII.

The Cheese Wheel. My second nose job job.

Zach was the only one there when I came in that first morning. The shop was still a hushed grey blue inside, the sun not yet high enough to make it through the front windows that looked out onto Jones, a typically narrow West Village street.

We were open but there weren't many customers yet. This was lucky, because it gave Zach time to teach me things. Cheese things.

I was incredibly nervous. Though I soon realized, in the light of Zach's easy smile, that this job was going to be completely different from my last. Working at Soft Soap had felt like working in a bad dream—a weird cubicled chattering bad dream—while working in the

Cheese Wheel felt *real*—you know, like I had always imagined a job to be. I mean, I was wearing an apron! Behind a counter! Serving customers! (At least I would be soon.) Customers who wanted to talk to me about products and not shoe sizes.

Music came to mind. (Of course.)

Who will buy? from *Oliver!*—that number when all the street merchants sing and dance below Oliver's balcony in the fancy London square.

(*Who will buy my sweet red roses? Two blooms for a penny.*)

Actually, a whole bunch of salespeople from musicals popped into my head: Barnaby and Cornelius from *Hello Dolly!*, Harold Hill from *The Music Man*, Luther Billis, the trinket soldier from *South Pacific*, Sweeney Todd, from, you know, *Sweeney Todd*.

The minute Sweeney Todd snuck in, I tried to shift gears—there's just something about stinky cheese and mutilated people that does not sit well on the old tumtum.

"The two main things you need to learn," Zach said, "are which cheeses are which—all the different types—and how to measure them."

I swallowed. There were literally hundreds of cheeses. The refrigerator cases were jammed with rounds and wedges, bars and slabs.

(*Will you buy any milk today, Mistress? Any milk today?*)

"Don't worry," Zach said, chuckling at my expression. "You'll be amazed how soon you pick up the popular types. Also, a lot of customers know what they want, and they'll point to it—'*that* Danish blue over there—'" He gave a quick nod of his head.

Which Danish blue?!

"Measuring takes a bit more of a knack," Zach said.

Great.

"First, you have to feel the whole cheese to get a sense of its 'BMI'. Body mass index." He winked, responding to my clueless face. (Zach was a winker.) "How heavy it is for its size. Like in humans. You need to figure out if you have a really muscle-y cheese—one that works out—or a couch potato cheese, light and fatty." He picked up a thick orange Port Salut. "You have to get a feel for the different cheeses. And then," his smile widened, "you guess."

I gulped. "Is there any other way? Besides guessing?"

"You can weigh the entire cheese, I suppose." He plopped the whole Port Salut on the metal scale. "And then you use math—you know math? Figure out the proper proportion. One-fifth? One-tenth? When you've got that," he moved the wire knife along the waxed surface, "you cut."

(*Knives, knives to grind. Any knives to grind.*)

The math route was easier for me than sensing BMI. I tried to think of each cheese as one big pie chart. Zach let me practice on some smaller pieces, runt slabs and ends, all the time giving me delicious little creamy bits to taste. "Here's a popular goat," he'd say. "Or try some Havarti."

After half an hour of this, I began to feel more confident. I was learning all kinds of cool stuff too, like what cheeses were best eaten with Madeira (whatever that was). Forty-five minutes later, after Deanna stopped by to give me a hug and a cappuccino (she brought one for Zach too), I actually felt *cool*—calm, hip, efficient. Sure, the actual cut—usually made by sliding a sharp wire through the center of the cheeses—was still nerve-wracking, but I was totally getting it.

Soon, I even heard the words, "who's the cute cheese chick?"

They came from a guy with shoulder-length black hair and a black shirt with a little white guitar on its chest.

"David, meet Celia," Zach said, as he fished some keys out of a big white mug that said "Who's Boss?" on one side. "Celia, meet Dave. You know Mr. Z., " he smirked, as he tossed the keys over, "he don't even trust those guitar guys to keep track of their own keys."

Dave smirked back, catching the keys; even I, as a new but completely with-it employee, smirked back. (Mr. Z., I figured was Mr. Zenia, Deanna's dad.)

(*Ripe strawberries ripe!*)

A few minutes after Dave left, the sun began casting bright rectangles over the store's aisles, Zach handed me a cut of freshly-delivered baguette, and Marcel breezed in.

I had always thought of Marcel as a really interesting guy, even kind of cute, with his midnight blue beret, tendrils of hennaed hair, dark heavy-lidded eyes. His nose was a bit on the long side, but it looked good on him, authentic.

"Good morning," I said cheerfully.

"And who are you, leetle girl?" Marcel snarled. "And why are you behind my counter dripping crumbs?"

"She's the new girl, remember?" Zach interjected. "Celia."

Marcel eyed me sourly. "Ah. Zee one zat gets zee job because she is friends with zee bossgirl. And what's zis, eh?" He picked up a blunt cheese knife, and flicked it into the tips of my hair.

I nearly dropped my wedge of baguette.

"Zee hair and zee cheese do not mix." He pulled off his dark beret to reveal his own hair, pasted down like a helmet. It didn't look exactly hennaed under there, just orange. To my horror, he now used the cheese knife to flick a huge cobwebby hairnet off of it.

"You will wear zee net," he said, holding the net like a dead limp spider's web, the dead limp *used* spider's web, over my head.

"Can't she just put her hair back?" Zach asked.

"In a ponytail?" I added, pulling my hair together into a thick bunch.

"Hmmm..." Marcel scowled down.

I normally hated wearing my hair in a pony tail. Without a distracting frame of hair, Hank looked humongous. But anything was better than Marcel's used hairnet—

"Zee hands," Marcel went on, irritably. "You must wash zee hands after you touch zee hair. And if it gets in zee way—zere!" He picked up an old blue coffee can by the cash register. It was filled with a tangle of funky hairnets.

"It won't get in the way," I said quickly.

"Hah!"

XXIII.

I put back zee hair. I washed zee hands. I even tried to laugh when Zach joked "zee hair and zee cheese—zey do not mix. As if you'd want them to!" But it was hard to recapture the cheeriness of my first couple of hours in the shop. (*Two blooms for a penny.*)

It wasn't just that I hated wearing my hair back. The store also got totally jammed and no one wanted any of the precut cheese. Oh no, they all wanted cheese that was freshly measured, freshly cut. Crazy cheeses too—Cabra al Vino, Sweet Gorgonzola, Red Leicester and Brunost (a hard brown Norwegian cheese whose name, Zach said, meant "brown cheese.")

In the face of the crowd, my sense of hip efficiency totally wilted. As I rushed to pick out and cut, and cut again, and pick out again (oops! Sorry!) and cut again, and wrap and take money and wrap and pick out and cut some more, I felt both awkward and bumbling.

Marcel, in the meantime, came and went, not, seemingly, bothered by the line of customers. He was managing the mail-order business down in the basement, Zach explained, rolling his eyes. "Working on that laptop takes oh so much time."

Marcel's mucking around in the basement irritated Zach, but I didn't mind, even if it did make us more rushed upstairs. Anything was better than having Marcel in the shop.

It wasn't just my hair, or my klutziness. What really seemed to infuriate him was the fact that I was Deanna's friend. He kept glaring at me and making remarks about "rich spies."

The one time he overheard me giving the customer *aged* manchego instead of *young*, he chuckled dismissively, "hah. Nobody care if zee *bossfriend* waste zee merchandise."

"Don't mind Marcel," Zach said after he went back downstairs. "It's not you he's mad at. It's Mr. Z. Marcel wanted to manage both stores. That way he thought he wouldn't need to work the counters at all, but Mr. Z. said Get More Guitars needed someone who actually knew guitars."

"That's where Dave is from, right? And all those other guys?"

We made these really great grilled panini, which were bought by customers, but had been given free to Dave and an assortment of other slightly hairy guys, and one bald one, who all wore the same black guitar-embossed t-shirts.

"That's right. Mr. Z. gives 'em free lunch as part of the job."

Technically, Mr. Z gave me free lunch too. But by the time my very late lunch break rolled around, the idea of putting one more piece of cheese near my face was sort of repugnant.

Even bread was losing its appeal.

The only thing that made sense was more cappuccino.

As I dragged myself down Jones Street to get some, I passed Get More Guitars. I looked through the window and saw two of the guys I'd made panini for earlier. Something about them made me think of Petry, even though they were older than him and not particularly good-looking. (One was the bald guy, and the other had kind of a tummy.) Maybe it was the way they held their guitars; there was something about their fingers—kind of fine and bony and strong all at the same time.

I reminded myself that I'd never actually seen Petry hold a guitar. I'd seen his hands moving up and down the keyboard though. That was in Chorus where he heard my voice all the time. And seemed to think it was terrific.

I felt suddenly embarrassed and happy and guilty and sad and angry all at once. How could Petry's dad not believe in him?

And what about me? What had I done to help him? Nothing.

Suddenly, even in my cheese daze, my need-for-caffeine daze, my first-day-of-work daze, I knew I had to change that.

But how?

XXIV.

I stepped into Get More Guitars, thinking about the way Maddy started a project, about how she'd get people talking, then riled up.

Of course, *her* projects were usually protests. *I* was trying to solve a crime. That would take a bit more finesse.

Smile a lot, I told myself.

Flirt.

Okay, okay. Forget about the flirting. (When you have a Hank, why bother?)

Just ask some questions, Celia.

I went up to the counter where a bald guy stood. He wore a name tag that said Luther.

"So, um, Luther—do you mind if I call you that?"

He smiled back at me. "No problem."

"So, um, you guys had a big robbery the other day, huh?"

It wasn't exactly *finessed*, but it was a start.

"Yeah, a Stratocaster, a beaut," Luther said.

I tried to stay innocent. "They know who took it?"

"Not sure yet," said Dave, stepping from a room behind the counter. "You're Celia, right? Hi."

"Come on, man. They got his ID—" Carl, the one with the tummy, a pale blond guy, said. (Clearly, he was not nearly so swift as Dave.)

"You can't believe it was him," Dave said.

"Boy sure likes a good guitar," Luther sighed.

"Yeah, but how would he even have known the guitar was here?"

"Didn't he come in that day?" Carl asked.

"The guy comes in most days," Luther sighed. "At least stands outside the window with those dogs of his."

"But he—that guy you're talking about—he wouldn't *steal* a guitar. You know that, right?" I tried.

"Boy sure wants a good guitar," Luther shrugged again.

Dave grinned. "That was one yummy panini, Celia. But I wouldn't talk about guitars to your man Marcel. He wanted to take us over, tell us zis and zat." He sneered. "It was his idea for Mr. Z. to get the Clapton to begin with. He thought we should have a showcase of famous guitars, like a little museum. Problem is I don't think Mr. Z. could actually bear to sell guitars like that. Like the Clapton. Mr. Z. was planning to take it home the day after it came into the shop."

I nodded slowly. "So whoever took it must have known the store pretty well?"

"Or been damn lucky."

As I was leaving Get More Guitars, I checked out the video camera (as in, stared up at it.)

116

It was black and silver and mounted on the wall, just like the one in the Cheese Wheel. It didn't scan or rotate. It just sat up there by the ceiling, mute, unblinking.

I turned to Luther. "How can they be so sure the video was right? I mean, if Petry, I mean, *that guy*, comes in here a lot, isn't it possible that there was film of him from earlier in the day? Maybe even earlier in the week?"

Luther sighed. "It's stamped on the footage. Says the hour and date right there."

"But isn't it weird it only got his back? I mean, the robber's back."

"It's not really aimed at the door; it's to protect the small stuff—CDs and electronic tuners. No one's going to put a whole guitar under their coat."

"Oh."

He chuckled. "It's mainly for show, to tell the truth. Nobody here even looks at the films. Only your buddy Marcel when he wants to act like the boss."

"Marcel," I whispered, pulling out my cell to check the time. My face must have turned green. They all laughed.

"Thanks a lot," I sighed.

"See ya."

I hurried back to the Cheese Wheel. With one last breath, and a really intense wish for the coffee I hadn't got, I stepped back into its moldy haze.

The Cheese Wheel was less crowded now at least. That made me hope that maybe I'd have a little time to investigate there too.

I did try. But whenever I asked Zach even the simplest question like 'hey Zach, wasn't there some robbery around here the other day?'

Marcel was right behind us. (Now that we had fewer customers, he seemed to be hanging around upstairs.)

"What is zis talking all zee time when zere are zee boxes to be unloaded, zee cheese to be measured, zee Parmesan to be grated? Even friends of zee boss can't sit and talk all day, eh? And zee pony tail," he pointed, "it is insufficient. Take one of zee hair nets. Now."

Truly despising him, I reached into the can by the cash register, hoping that one of the bottom ones might be somehow less used, at least less *recently* used.

I could feel invisible head lice diving onto my scalp even before I picked one of the wormy nets out from the can. But I wanted to keep this job, so I stretched one over my head, flattening both my hair and the small bit of ego I had left.

"And now, get to zose boxes. And you, Zachariah—see to zee Parmegiano."

"What boxes?" I asked dully.

"In zee storage closet, eh, Bossfriend?"

I stepped to a little door at the side of the counter area, the door to a large cupboard. A small key hung on a nail to its side. I took it down and was just wiggling it in the lock when Marcel went gonzo.

"Idiote. Bête." He didn't even seem to mind the people in the shop. "Ferme la porte, shut it, what are you doing? Salot—"

"You said the storage closet," I protested.

"Zee storage closet in zee *back* of zee shop." He led me by the arm through the aisles. "*Ici*, by zee cookbooks, zee magazine." He opened up a huge closet behind some French doors. "You see—zee boxes of pasta, zee crackers."

"He's not normally so crazed," Zach said, when I returned to the cash register. "Can't quite see what's got into the man."

I thought of Ms. Deronda, then of Larry, the Soft Soap guy, then of Petry's dad, and how furious I seemed to make them all. "I sometimes have this effect on people."

"It's not you," Zach said, but somehow I couldn't believe that.

XXV.

By the time I got home, I felt more tired than I had ever felt—tired of work, tired of life, very—*very*—tired of cheese.

I also smelled horrible. Like a Camembert that was so ripe it had mutated. (The only parts of me that were bearable were my underarms, mainly because they still held a residue of deodorant.)

I smelled horrible even after a shower, a bath, and another shower. The water, the soap, the bubble bath, could not wash the odor away. It had gotten into my pores, my oversized nostrils, my nervous system.

A lesson: if you love cheese, do not work in a cheese store, especially not a good cheese store. A good cheese store will not only destroy your love of a few common kinds of cheeses—let's say, cheddar and muenster—it will destroy your love of every kind of cheese you could possibly come across.

As I thought about all the homework I should start (since I was supposed to be back at the Cheese Wheel all the next day), the idea of earning money for a nose job seemed less and less desirable, especially when compared to the option of just doing Brad's homework. Maybe I could tell him I'd do all his college work too, and even, I don't know, his taxes for the rest of his life.

Then would he at least make me an understudy?

Or maybe, I thought dismally, I should skip the understudy part, and just do taxes, sitting in a basement, behind a curtain, with a veil over my face, singing only in my head and in the shower, and never ever *ever* eating cheese.

The culmination of all that was bad came the next afternoon down in the basement, the "mail order" section of the Cheese Wheel, which also held the cold storage. Zach had sent me down there to bring up a large gouda.

I don't much like basements, especially not city basements that are full of cheese, so when Zach asked me to go down there, I told myself I'd make it super-fast.

But there were lots of shelves down there, each one full of big gouda-like cheese wheels. Some were covered in red wax, some yellow, some black. Some of the cheeses seemed as big as tires, others more like hubcaps.

Concentrating on the hubcaps—no way could I even lift the tire ones—I cursed myself for not asking Zach for more details. He'd said something about "aged" and "prima donna," but the words I needed were the "big red one on the top row of the closest shelf, third from the right."

To tell the truth, the basement at the Cheese Wheel wasn't so bad for a basement. Mr. Z. or Marcel—whoever made decisions about these things—had had the place painted white. It was also pretty clean, except for a few sheets of packaging cardboard on one side of the floor, and a very messy worktable by one wall. On the worktable was a lap-top and a jigsaw of receipts, order forms, used coffee cups, cigarette wrappers (the French kind), an ash tray overflowing with scrunched and bent cigarette butts, and—I noticed when I rested some wheels of cheese on the table—several big shards of broken plastic.

Wait a second. The plastic came from what looked like a split video cassette. It was smaller than our old VHS tapes, but there were loops of black video tape curling out of it. Big shiny loops.

I looked to the wastebasket at the side of the table. It had cigarette wrappers too, and mixed in with those, snips of shiny plastic. More bits of video tape.

I wondered if you could see what was on a video by just looking at the tape. I was about to check, when—

"Bossfriend," hissed behind me.

I jumped.

"What are you doing down here, Bossfriend?" Marcel stepped closer now, so close that I could smell him, so close that I could smell practi-cally nothing *but* him. It was a smell of cigarettes mixed with cheese. "You want to be alone with me, eh?"

"No, I...um...Zach asked me to get a gouda."

"You are in luck there, ma fille. Because I am very gouda."

Laughing at his stupid joke, he put his arms around me, leaning his beret into my neck. His touch bristled with whiskers, wool, orangi-fied hair, everything sharp and hard except for his lips—eeeuuuwww—which he pressed forcefully into mine. In spite of the pressure, they had a clammy softness, like the underbelly of a snake in a tobacco field.

The genes I shared with Maddy instantly exploded. I pushed him hard with both hands, then stamped on one foot. "Get away from me!" I screamed the second my mouth was free.

"Aiee!" he cried, collapsing onto one knee. "You lame me! Merde! Why, you silly girl?"

"Why?!" I panted. "You grabbed me, you jerk."

"It was a blague, a joke. Why would I grab a little girl like you? My little Bossfriend?"

"I am not your Bossfriend," I said angrily. "You're the boss around here. But you know what? Not of me. I am getting out of this place right now."

"Please, Celia. I'm so sorry."

"So *now* you know my name?"

"It was an accidente, ma faute. Please accept my terrible pardon."

He stopped rubbing his foot and, still bent on one knee, pressed his hands together in a prayer pose. It was disgusting,

"I quit," I said. I pulled off the hairnet and stuck it over one of his yucky fingernails. "All I want is to be paid, paid for the whole stupid weekend."

Marcel limped up the basement stairs. I followed, clacking my feet as loudly as possible. Marcel slid by the confused Zach, and took two hundred dollar bills from the cash register. "For today and yesterday," he said. "You can forget zee tax."

"I only make ten an hour," I said, taking only one of the hundreds and reaching past him for three twenties. "And I don't cheat my best friend's dad."

Marcel wiped his forehead. His face was covered with sweat, abject creamy sweat. "You want some cheese?" he whispered. "An assortement?"

"Keep your damn cheese."

When I got home, I took an endless shower. If Maddy had been there, she would have shouted something about droughts through the bathroom door. But I couldn't think about droughts just then. I only wanted to get clean.

By the time I logged on, Brad was already on my case.

Boymeetsgirl17: Hey Blu, number 1?

He didn't even pretend to do his own homework anymore. I tried to remind myself that he was my only chance for a part in a big televised musical, my only chance for a part in life!—especially now that I'd quit the Cheese Wheel. Even so, it was hard to feel enthusiastic.

Bluesong: just a sec.

Then Deanna came on.

**Pinkwstripes: i dropped by the Cheese Wheel.
They said u quit???**

Oh crap. What was I going to tell her?

I was still shaking inside. Even after the endless shower, I could smell a mixture of cheese and cigarette on my skin, just above what seemed to be a thick layer of guilt. It was as if a part of me felt like the whole thing with Marcel was somehow my fault, even though I knew it wasn't, that it couldn't be.

Luckily, Deanna didn't wait for my reply.

Pinkwstripes: haven't gotten my guitar back yet. Told my dad we should definitely press charges.

Wait a second. Deanna and her father were going to press charges? Against Petry?

Everything scrambled inside me, scrambled more. I couldn't think straight. All I knew for certain was that when Deanna talked about pressing charges against Petry, I didn't want to even *talk* to her, much less *be* like her. No way was I going to tell her about Marcel; no way was I going to get him into trouble, even if he deserved it; no way was I going to be the kind of person who ruined other people's lives.

My reaction didn't make a huge amount of sense. Petry was a really good guy, Marcel was a total jerk. But Deanna was totally bumming me out and, for the moment, I couldn't seem to think much farther than that.

XXVI.

"No, I didn't leave it at home," Petry said as I stepped into the school doorway. He was talking to the security guard.

"You lost it?" the guard asked.

"No, I didn't lose it. I mean, yes, I lost it," Petry mumbled.

It was strange the way I kept running into him at the school's front door. Not that I minded meeting up with him. It's just that every time Petry and I met at the door, there was also a security guard there, which kind of brought the moment down.

I walked with him to the attendance office to get a day pass.

"The police won't give me my old ID, and the school hasn't gotten around to issuing a new one," he said glumly.

"What a drag."

He shrugged.

"Did your dad tell you I called?"

His face turned hard. "Trying to get more evidence for your friend?"

"Petry, no!"

He shook hair out of eyes that looked hooded, skeptical, hurt.

"I called because I wanted to tell you that I'm your alibi," I tried.

"What do you mean?"

"Because we were talking all the time you were supposedly—"
what was that word they always used for Maddy?— "*allegedly* robbing
the store."

He stopped walking. I could see that he was thinking back to our
call. "You're right."

But instead of getting excited, he sighed and started towards the
office again. The jumble of students to our sides were already staring;
now the kids in front stared too, turning back to get a better view. I tried
to pretend I didn't notice; Petry kept his own gaze trained on the floor.

"Don't you see?" I whispered. "I called your home number almost
exactly at the time stamped on the video. I tried to tell your dad, but
he said—"

"That I had our phone on forward. Yeah, I did."

"You can do that?"

"Lucky guy, huh?"

"But where were you? I know you weren't breaking any glass."

"The glass was cut, not broken."

I tried not to think about how Petry would know that. It was not
because he'd been on the scene, I told myself sternly.

"But then how did you—I don't mean *you*—how did *the burglar* get
through that metal gate?"

"The lock was picked," he shrugged. "Opened anyway."

"But wouldn't I have heard you pushing the gate open?"

A vein tensed in Petry's pale neck. He pushed his hair from a face
that looked pained, angry.

"Is that the only reason you think I didn't do it? Because you didn't hear it?"

"No, I was just saying—I was just—"

"You were just trying to help your friend land me in jail. She's pushing for that."

"I wasn't—I wouldn't!"

"What I wonder is why you called me to begin with."

"It was that stupid job. You know that, right?"

I wanted to grab his sleeve, make him stop, make him look at me. But he had slipped through the office door. I couldn't follow him in there.

I walked on through the hallway, face down. The people who had been staring at Petry and me together now just stared at me. Even with my head down, I could see the "perfect girls," Jessica, Emma, Tracy. Tracy wore blue leggings that morning and a little striped mini, Jessica a super-tight tank top. Their noses were short and cute, their ears clung to the sides of their heads, their pouty lips were lined with deep red lipliner, their brains with smugness.

They were walking with Brad, Jessica on one side, Emma on the other, Tracy on the other side of Jessica. (But probably not for long. I could see those smooth blue legs angling across Jessica's path.)

I felt Hank swelling with tears, and I cursed myself, but not, this time, because Hank would turn red. Hank felt like the least of my problems, like one tiny—okay, one fairly large—imperfection in the huge mound of imperfections that made up the rest of me.

XXVII.

I saw Petry repeatedly that day, but he never saw me back. I mean, he probably did *see* me—someone with a Hank in the middle of their face is hard to miss—but he refused to *seem to* see me, if you know what I mean. So that even when I tried to tell him—with my eyes—that I really did believe in him, I had no sense that I was getting through.

Deanna, for her part, glared at him every chance she got.

All that was bad enough, and then came Pre-Cal. Tracy, Emma and Jessica were hanging outside the door, gabbing with Brad when I walked in. Tracy, Emma and Jessica acted like they didn't even know me (*fine!*), though Brad gave a slight lift of his eyebrows. (*Ha!*)

When Brad sauntered to his seat—do all tennis players have that walk?—he even gave me one of those little waist-high waves.

I tried not to blush. I tried not to immediately start singing inside.

Then Ms. Geller called the class to order and the reasons for Brad's friendliness became horribly clear.

"As all of you who have given due attention to the syllabus duly posted online for this class will know, we are due to have our first big chapter test this coming Monday. Those who have done their home-work on a regular basis should have nothing to worry about on this test. Those of you who have been remiss in your homework assignments, however—and you know who you are—"

The rest of Ms. Geller's words passed in a sick blur. I could feel Brad turning towards me, I could feel his beautiful smile—the small, bashful version—sneaking into my airspace like a drone missile.

I tried not to look at him directly. Yet I couldn't help but see him at my side, visible just around the big fleshy blur of Hank. Did Brad really think I'd help him cheat? On a *test?*

If not, then why was he smiling at me like that? And why was it creeping me out?

The streets were wet after school. It had rained hard just before ninth; the air was still grey and damp, the overhangs of the shops on Bleecker Street dripping. Rain drops are fine, but drips from New York City awnings—not so great. Let's just say, pigeons are very busy in NYC. Deanna and I were careful where we walked.

"What I can't believe is the way he just acts like nothing's wrong," Deanna groused, jumping over the dark pool at one curbside. (We had to watch out for water on the street too. I'm not just talking pigeons here.)

I tried to focus on Deanna but my mind was full of Brad. He had followed me out of Pre-Cal, and then, just before he'd disappeared into the girl moat (Trina, the cheerleader, had joined Tracy, Emma, and Jessica, who'd been waiting for him in the hall), he'd called out, "Celia!" making a little 'call me' gesture.

"It's so crazy. He didn't just steal an expensive guitar, he stole a symbol of a whole generation. And he doesn't even act like he's sorry."

"Wait a sec. You're talking about Petry, right?" I shook myself into the moment. "Why *should* he be sorry?"

"What do you mean, 'why should he be sorry?' He stole my guitar!"

I sighed. "Except that he didn't."

"Come on, Celia. I know you like the guy, but the police arrested him."

"The police aren't right about everything."

"You're just trying to act like your sister."

My face flushed. "I am not just trying to act like my sister. I just think the police are totally wrong here. Look, let's drop it, okay?"

We silently fumed past Jones.

And talk about fumes. I could make out the stench of the Cheese Wheel even from around the corner—Hank could anyway—a cloud of fermented butterfat.

Maybe Deanna could smell it too. Or maybe it was just the closeness of the shop that brought it to her mind. "So, now you're not even going to try to earn the money to get your nose fixed?" she said. "You're just giving up?"

"A job takes a lot of time. And I was kind of hoping," I sighed guiltily, "that maybe Brad will give me some kind of part, even *with* Hank."

"Speaking of Brad," Deanna cut in. "He came over to me in the hall today and said that he was having this pre-pre-audition thing soon, and wanted me to be sure to come. Can you believe it? He said he'd been watching me in the hall for a long time and was sure I'd be just perfect for something."

A green lump filled my chest. Deanna had never taken one bit of interest in theater. Maybe a couple of times in middle school she had worked on costumes, but mainly that was because I was already acting and her mom had pushed her to get involved too. (Plus they'd let her use duct tape.)

As for singing—it just wasn't her thing. She hardly sang 'happy birthday' and even that was off-key.

I felt the green lump swell around my heart and stomach. I also felt Deanna's eyes on me. I made myself smile. "Brad offered you a part? Wow."

"Isn't that weird? Kind of cool though. He didn't know exactly what it would be, only, he said, something fun."

Did Brad also say (I wanted to ask) that since the guitar was stolen, he'd suddenly realized that you had a super famous model for a mom and that your dad had produced music for just about everybody in the business and that the TV people were sure to love all that?

Did Brad also say (my angry brain went on), that he always thought you were kind of strange and dumpy but now that he knew your parents were famous he suddenly noticed how cool you were?

I stared down at a muddy rivulet making its way through a crack in the sidewalk.

"You're not going to get all jealous on me?" Deanna groaned.

"No way," I lied. "I just never thought you wanted to be in a musical."

"I didn't know that I did either. But now it sounds like a blast. With it being on TV and everything. And maybe it could help me start selling my purses and stuff. Maybe the TV people would film them. And you know, Ceel, if I get in good with Brad, maybe I could get him to give you a part too."

We stood at Deanna's door. Her twin brothers' drawings of big bloodshot monster eyes peered out the downstairs windows. Inside hot chocolate and Vogues would be waiting.

Deanna leaned on the bell. "Bisfiniditel?" gurgled a voice.

"It's me," she shouted.

The lock buzzed.

"You coming?"

"Can't."

"You're sure?"

"Yup. Sorry."

I charged away from the door, nearly running into a guy with a baseball cap and big camera. "Is that the house where the Clapton guitar was stolen?" he asked.

"It wasn't stolen from a house," I said, hating reporters who treated my friends like celebrities and got them fun parts in TV musicals.

Stop it, Celia, I told myself. Maybe being in the musical *would* get attention for Deanna's purses. Maybe she secretly *had* always wanted to act and sing. Maybe she *would* be able to get Brad to give you a part.

As I stood by the curb, a cab jolted through a huge trough of rainwater (what I hoped was rainwater) and sprayed me with dark grey jets of the stuff.

Just what I needed.

I did Brad's homework as usual that night. After I sent him number 10, he wrote back asking for my cell number because he said he wanted to call me.

A part of me got giddy and excited even though I was pretty sure of what he wanted to talk about.

"Hey, Ceel," he said, "about this chapter test."

Those weren't exactly the words I ached to hear, but I was ready.

"I could tutor you," I offered. "I know the stuff pretty well and—"

"Oh yeah, sure. You're so good in math, it's incredible," Brad said, "but you know, I'm awfully busy for tutoring, what with this TV musical...." His voice trailed off suggestively.

"Um," I replied.

"So, maybe we can meet tomorrow and, like, plan—"

"Plan?"

"For the, like, chapter test. You know. How we're going to handle it. I was thinking...you might want a part in the musical too, right?"

Was Brad asking me to help cheat on the Pre-Cal test in exchange for a part?

"Don't you, like, sing or something?" he went on.

Did he really think I would cheat in order to get a part?

Would I?

As my thoughts scattered in about two hundred and fifty directions, I became conscious of a bass beat beneath my feet; the pizza parlor had turned up its boom box again.

With the sound came a flashback of Brad's hand, that beautifully tanned hand, slipping a green beer bottle under his jacket.

"Brad, there's someone at the door." I stamped my feet loudly, hoping it sounded like knocking. "Look, I'll see you tomorrow, okay."

After I clapped down the lid of my phone, I sat on my bed, massively depressed.

I listened to the beat below my feet, trying to make out the melody, but all I could catch was the dull dumdiddy of the bass. Where was a song when you needed one?

XXVIII.

I kept my distance from everyone the next day.

I knew Deanna's routines, so it wasn't hard to avoid her. I just took different halls and stairways than usual. I felt kind of guilty about that, but I also knew that avoiding her was probably the only way we could sidestep a major fight.

Brad was also easy to steer clear of. All I had to do was to keep an eye out for the girl moat.

Petry wasn't actually on my list of people to stay away from. Okay, let's be honest; I hoped that if I weren't joined at the hip with Deanna he might approach me himself.

I really wanted to talk to him, but I also didn't want to be too obvious about it.

It worked. He caught up with me in a back hall, trying to smile, but looking terrible, exhausted, stressed. "Look, I'm really sorry I've been such a bummer. This has been a hard few days."

"I bet," I said.

"And, uh…do you have fifth period lunch?"

We walked fast and a little apart as we left school, trying, unsuc-cessfully, to avoid a zillion stares. Was Deanna watching? Brad?

A part of me didn't want to know. Another part of me surrepti-tiously scanned the crowd.

There was Brad all right. His glow was hard to miss, especially when haloed by the combined glossiness of Tracy, Emma, Jessica.

A part of me went momentarily ballistic. Probably they would all get to be in the musical—Tracy, Emma, Jessica, even Deanna—with-out having to cheat or anything.

Then another part of me looked over at Petry. Petry, who was fight-ing to clear his name!

Then a fourth or fifth part of me (a very sneaky part) wondered whether my friendship with Petry might not help me get into the musical too in some weird way. Maybe it would make Brad think that I was interesting. Maybe the TV people would want to highlight me as the girl who was friends with a famous guitar thief.

(Except that Petry wasn't a famous guitar thief. He wasn't any kind of guitar thief.)

(Oh yeah, and what about the fact was that Brad was probably not going to even talk to me, much less cast me, unless I helped him "han-dle" the math test?)

I shook my head, shut my eyes, tried to just walk along as one whole person, all the different parts glued together.

After what seemed like ages, we crossed the street that seemed to officially divide school from the rest of New York City. Petry sighed. "I'm sorry that I've been such a jerk."

"You haven't been," I said.

"And your friend—"

"She's the one being a jerk," I muttered, then cringed inside. Deanna was my best friend.

"Hey, I don't blame her. If I thought I was going to get Eric Clapton's guitar and some prick came along and stole it, I'd be really mad too."

"Yeah, but you *didn't* steal it."

"They *did* find my ID."

I didn't add, "and the video of you," but the words hung in the air between us.

We walked fast—school lunch breaks are short—ending up at a little place called the Punjabi Tea House. Taxi cabs lined up outside, cab drivers lined up inside. The food smelled deliciously spicy and warm; the service, geared towards the illegally parked, was super quick.

We sat by the window, shielded by fogged-up glass and a constantly shifting line of turbans, their colors ranging from a beautiful deep pink to a beautiful dove grey. There was no one else from school. It was terrific.

Petry dipped a somosa into an electric green sauce, bit into it hungrily.

Me too. The curried smells were a perfect antidote to the undercurrent of mold that, even after a couple of days away from the Cheese Wheel, still dogged my oversized nostrils.

After a few chews, Petry seemed to unwind a little. "I've been racking my brain but I just can't figure out how they got that stuff. The ID's different. It must have fallen out of my pocket—when I got home that night, there was a rip in my pants. But the video—" He shook his head.

"So, where were you? You know, when I got you on the phone?"

He laughed. "Hunkered down behind some pots and pans."

"Pots and pans?"

"Yeah, and sitting on top of some cooking magazines. At that little cooking store. Cheese store really. In the Village. The Cheese Wheel? You know it?"

"I worked there all last week-end."

"Really?" he laughed. "That's the gig I was going to tell you about. Remember? I didn't say it at the time because—" He dipped another somosa into the sauce. "I guess I wanted an excuse to talk to you again."

I felt my cheeks heat up (and not because of the spices.) "Why were *you* hanging out at the Cheese Wheel?"

"It was my brother, Harter. He's in second grade. He'd finished his homework and wanted to go over there to check out some cookbooks and," he grinned, "sniff chocolate."

"Sniff chocolate?"

"It's not what it sounds like." He laughed. "He wanted to get a better sense of the different kinds—Belgian, Kenyan, Colombian—"

"Aren't they all wrapped in cellophane?"

"Yeah," he chuckled. "And they all smell like cheese. Kind of terrible. He says no one should ever buy baking chocolate in that store, by the way."

"Your brother buys baking chocolate?"

"Look, he's just a kid," Petry said, offering me the dish of spinach and chick peas. "And he loves to cook. He's just crazy about it. Watches cooking shows, reads cookbooks, invents recipes. And his cooking actually tastes great most of the time.

"Most of the time?"

"He went through a prosciutto phase that got a little gross—"

"Your seven-year-old brother cooks with prosciutto?"

"Not anymore, thank God."

"Let me get this straight. You and your brother were in the Cheese Wheel at 7:42. So you couldn't have taken the guitar then. Didn't you tell your parents?"

"I did, but they weren't exactly thrilled that we were in the Cheese Wheel either."

"Your parents let you get arrested because they weren't thrilled you were in the Cheese Wheel?"

"It's not really like that," Petry sighed. "I got arrested because I got arrested. As for the rest—my dad doesn't like Harter cooking so much. Here, you want some more of this spinach stuff?" He pushed the dish closer to me, sighing again.

"Harter's a little overweight," Petry continued. "A lot of kids his age are. But my dad thinks it's because of the cooking."

"But you took him to sniff chocolate anyway?

"Yeah—"

"And that's where you were when we talked on the phone?"

"Yes, while I was sitting on the cookbooks, and Harter was sniffing the chocolates. I think he did finally get that guy, the nice one, to unwrap some for him."

"That's Zach."

"The tan one? Without the beret?"

I nodded. Petry looked at his watch, then back to me. We got up reluctantly. I wiped my mouth one last time with my napkin, then felt stupidly prim and embarrassed.

He waited for me to slip out of my seat ahead of him, his head slightly bowed.

I angled through the line of cab drivers and then Petry was somehow in front of me again, holding the door open. I tried to speed through it, without tripping.

We both took big gulps of the cold, fresh-for-New-York-City air.

"Wait a second," I said as my brain re-activated. "If your brother was with you the whole time, why didn't *he* tell your folks?"

"He did, but my dad doesn't believe him. He won't flat out say it, but he doesn't."

"Why not?"

Petry stuck his hands deep in his pockets, hunching his shoulders. "I guess we've kind of shot our wad there."

"What do you mean?"

"I'm not perfect, okay?"

"Who is?"

"The thing is—" He kept walking, a flush of red at his neck— "I lie sometimes. To my parents. We've both lied actually, my brother and me both, and now—"

I tried to keep my face open, to not look judgmental or anything, but my brain started a downward spiral: Petry *lied*; Petry had *lied*. Did that mean that he really did take the guitar?

Then I caught myself. I thought of the times I'd told my mom that I couldn't hear the boom boxes downstairs, or that I'd done all my homework, or that I was coming straight home—

"People lie sometimes. Even the government," I said. "You should hear my sister."

Petry laughed. "Your sister's that girl Maddy, right? Boy, she used to terrify me. Always making people sign these petitions, and I remember once when her hair was so *dirty*—"

Everybody remembered that time with Maddy's hair.

"But what about you and... Harter—" (What kind of a name was Harter? Come to think of it, what kind of name was Petry?)

"So, Harter was supposed to be going to these special conditioning classes on Saturday mornings. Because of his weight. But he really hated the classes. All the gymnastics stuff freaked him out."

"Poor kid."

"And yours truly was supposed to take him."

"Bummer."

"You're telling me. He'd whine and moan and try to bribe me," Petry grimaced.

"He has money?"

"With his allowance."

"You didn't take his allowance?!"

"No! He only gets like a dollar a week. Anything more and they're afraid he'll buy truffles."

"Or prosciutto."

"Yeah," he laughed. "He got so upset that he and I...well, we just kind of started doing other things."

"Other than going to gymnastics?"

He nodded. "I *would* try to get him to exercise. We'd jog around Washington Square, or along the river. Other times I'd get him to dance or do push-ups."

"He'd do push-ups on the street?"

"Nah, we'd go jam at the music school. In the East Village. There are open sessions Saturdays."

"Your brother didn't mind doing push-ups while you jammed?"

Petry's overlapping tooth showed when he laughed, but in a weirdly cozy way. "It wasn't like we made fun of him. We'd usually get down and do some too."

"He didn't feel stupid?"

"No way. He got so into it he started making little treats the night before. You know, for the band."

He looked up. We were across the street from school, still on neutral ground. He set his feet more squarely on the pavement, as if not quite willing to move on.

"I didn't just drag him along to whatever I wanted either." Petry's face tightened. This seemed to be a point he'd made before. "We went to that big Chocolate Show when it was here, and once to the Natural History Museum."

"When they had their exhibition on chocolate?"

"Okay," he laughed. "But Harter did get fitter. And it also turned him on to the idea of cooking for other people. Before, when he made muffins, he'd eat half of them himself, mainly so he could justify making a new batch. Now—"

We had crossed the street. The glass doors of the school were still halfway down the block, but invisible walls seemed to rapidly descend around us.

"My dad found out," Petry said, voice lowered. "He was furious."

"Because of the lying?"

He nodded. "Also, he'd paid for the gymnastics lessons. So I had to pay him back. That's another reason that he doesn't take my word about the guitar. He thinks I'd try to sell it to get some cash. As if I'd ever sell Eric Clapton's guitar."

Every kid in the block seemed to pick up on those three last words despite Petry's whisper. The eavesdropping was so intense it seemed to hum.

"So, how are you going to prove it?" I whispered back.

Petry looked down at a stain on the sidewalk, rubbing it with the toe of his sneaker. The movement made me think of his knobbly knees.

I'd only seen them in gym, but I remembered their wiry paleness. They were knees that were usually wore blue jeans, I guessed, not exposed to the sun (or anything else much either.) Not like Brad's knees, which were tan and smooth and could be seen 24/7 on the tennis team website.

Brad. Brad who wanted me to help him "handle" the math test; Brad who people only stared at in order to drool over.

"There's got to be a way to prove the *truth*," I whispered, my mind darting crazily from Brad to math—to proofs and theorems, Geometry and Logic, Trig and *Pre-Cal*—which brought me back to Brad again. (Ugh.)

"You'd think so," Petry sighed.

XXIX.

I purposely went late to Pre-Cal, so that I'd only have time to scurry to my seat and muck around with my notebooks looking flustered. This was not ideal, but it did give me an excuse not to immediately respond to the little notes Brad kept nudging onto the side of my desk . ("Hey Ceeeeelia!" and "We gotta talk!!!!")

My brain started singing *"I'm gonna wash that man right out of my hair,"* but all that did was make me think of how much I would give up to play Nellie Forbush in a televised *South Pacific.*

I told myself that I wouldn't even be the one doing the cheating. I'd just be helping out my fellow student.

Right.

Nellie Forbush sure wouldn't do it. Or Maria. Or Mary Poppins,

Still, I didn't have the nerve to write a big 'NO WAY' on one of Brad's notes. Or even to totally ignore him. Instead, I kept giving him quick helpless smiles, as in 'hey, I gotta focus here.'

When the bell rang, I ran.

I had a free the next period and went to the school library. That was the one place I was sure not to see either Brad or Deanna. For extra safety, I hunkered down behind a tall shelf labeled 'Geology.'

What was that saying of my mom's? She had a zillion. 'Between a rock and a hard place.'

It wasn't actually a saying, it was a description: it described what it was like to be in a difficult situation. Like I was just then, hiding out from my best friend and the boy I'd been trying to impress all semester.

Between a rock and a hard place. (Also, in this case, between some geology books and the floor.)

And then there was the whole question of Petry. And not just the question of how his knees could be so knobbly.

Or what made his hands so intriguing. He really did had very intriguing hands. You could see the tendons extend all the way up his arms.

He also had that cozily toothy smile.

And he didn't even seem to notice Hank.

So, how could I help him?

I could only come up with two possibilities. One was to persuade Deanna to persuade her dad not to press charges. Maybe I could even talk to Mr. Z. myself. I pictured myself in Deanna's wood-paneled library, arguing Petry's innocence. In my daydream, Mr. Z., in blue jeans and wire-rimmed glasses, nodded intently, just on the point of agreeing with me, when Deanna burst in, purple bangs shaking with rage: "how dare you?" she would shriek. "That Eric Clapton guitar was worth a lot. I might have even learned to play it some day!"

The other choice was to uncover the truth. If we could prove that Petry was innocent, then no one would have to beg Mr. Z not to press charges. Then Deanna would probably even like Petry. (But only as a friend, of course.)

Then everything would be wonderful.

Except, *duh*—I gathered up my backpack to get to A.P. Euro—I still wouldn't have money or a nose job or much of a chance for a part in the musical.

Deanna was waiting for me at my locker at the end of the day. She didn't mention that she hadn't seen me all day; I didn't mention that I had hid out from her. Instead, we tried to act as if everything was normal, our mutual miffed-ness a festering boil that we were each careful not to poke. This meant that we could not talk about Petry, Brad, the Eric Clapton guitar, or the pre-pre audition meeting.

"So why did you quit the Cheese Wheel?" Deanna asked as we took the turn onto Bleecker. "You never really said."

The Cheese Wheel was another topic I would have just as soon avoided. (I should have been pre-emptive, started up on something like shoes.)

"I got totally sick of the smell," I tried.

"I thought you liked cheese."

"It's okay for a couple of minutes, but all day—"

"Oh yeah. I hadn't thought of that."

"And Marcel is kind of a pain."

"Really? He always seems so cool. He's like the world's biggest cheese expert."

"He's not so cool as a boss."

"He's quitting too, did you know? My dad was going on about it. Like in a week or something."

Marcel was quitting? Was he still mad because they never let manage him Get More Guitars? Or was it me? Maybe he thought it was better to quit than have me sue him—

After I split from Deanna, I slowly made my way down Morton Street. There wasn't a film crew today. No plastic leaves, no black cables, no silver vans. I unlocked the downstairs door to my building and climbed up the stairs. Waiting in the stairwell was a neighbor whose hair was wedged into pink foam curlers, that were, in turn, crammed under a paisley scarf. One leg was covered with a white plaster cast, her pink and black flowered pants slit down that side.

"Hi Mrs. Gudge."

The woman had a large puffy bulldog squeezed under one arm; her other hand clung to the banister.

"It's his poor legs that are the trouble," she said, her face damp with worry.

"You want me to take him out?"

"Do you mind? The poor dear's about to burst."

I stared into the sad and slightly bloodshot eyes of the snuffling bulldog, who, frankly, always looked like he was about to burst.

"Let me just put my books down."

"You'll have to carry him down the stairs. It's his legs."

I groaned inside. "Just a sec," I said.

"I've got newspaper," she called as I stepped into the apartment.

Oh yes. Newspaper.

I didn't mind helping Mrs. Gudge; I didn't even really mind the newspaper part. What bothered me was the idea of picking up Buster.

The sad bloodshot eyes were probably his most attractive feature. He also had a spittle-draped mouth, crisscrossed teeth, and a flabby pink belly that hung loosely between squat, thick-clawed legs.

"Don't bite me, Buster," I whispered as I bent down over that soulful face "Or…splat." Then placed my hands below his belly and rump. I was amazed to find that they were totally soft—flabby, but warm and dry. Yes, he weighed a lot, but I could also somehow feel gratitude mixed with the poundage.

"You're a good girl, Celia," Mrs. Gudge said.

I blushed. A part of my brain had already vaulted to thoughts of Petry and how he got paid for walking dogs. I knew it was ridiculous to get excited. Mrs. Gudge could not afford to pay anybody for anything, and I certainly wasn't about to ask her.

I carried Buster quickly down the stairs, through the front door, and put him down on the sidewalk. For a dog about to burst, he didn't seem very keen on being outside.

"Come on, Buster." I said, trying to tug him from the front door.

(*In every job that must be done, there is an element of fun, you find the fun and snap! the job's a game.*)

Oh-oh. And now, my brain was being weird again.

(*And every task you undertake…becomes a piece of cake. A lark! A spree! It's very clear to see…*)

"Come on, Buster," I tugged. But the dog seemed rooted to the square of sidewalk right in front of our door.

"Your mom's just inside." I tried, bending down. "Please," I patted.

Bloodshot eyes looked up dutifully. Stubby legs took a few stiff steps. "There's a good boy."

(*…that a spoonful of sugar makes the medicine go down, the medicine go dow-own, medicine go down.*)

As I waited for Buster to get down, further down, to business, the part of my brain that wasn't being Mary Poppins contemplated the news that Marcel was quitting.

I thought of how he had grabbed me. It still made me tremble inside.

But it was just so bizarre. Marcel didn't even seem to like me, much less find me attractive. Why would he jump me like that?

Buster turned in a slow trembling circle. (*A robin feathering his nest…has very little time to rest.*)

My mind too seemed to go in circles. Until everything clicked into place.

I had been looking at the worktable when Marcel made his pass, the worktable with the broken videocassette! I had been checking out the wastebasket too, with all the clipped snips of video tape!

(*The medicine go dow-own, medicine go down.*)

No wonder Marcel grabbed me. It wasn't that he was overcome by my looks; it was to make me *stop looking*. The whole thing was one big diversionary tactic.

For a brief second, I felt a huge wave of...disappointment.

Marcel's pass had been really gross. Yet there had also been something kind of...flattering.

Flattering?! Celia! The guy was a complete criminal.

Criminal....

Wait a second....

In the midst of my revelation, I looked down at Buster who was now quivering with alertness, his bottom fangs standing at attention.

A pack of dogs was coming down the street—

"Hey! I was hoping you'd be out," Petry said. "You live around here, right?"

"Yeah, just here," I colored, conscious suddenly that my building was the only really rundown one on the block.

Petry didn't seem to notice. He just stood there beaming, dogs jostling about his legs.

"So, are these your dogs then? I mean, your, um—"

"Walkees," Petry grinned.

There were seven of them, ranging from tall and pointy to short and schnauzery—

"Hey guys, relax!" Petry gently tugged the band of leashes. "Calm down! *Charlie!*"

Slowly, jaggedly, the dogs grew "calm," which meant that instead of *noisily* jostling like wildebeests at the back of a herd, they *quietly* jostled like wildebeests at the back of a herd.

"Who's this?" Petry smiled, nodding at Buster.

"He's my neighbor's dog. The two of them have bad legs."

"Cute little fellow." Petry bent down to scratch Buster's head.

"Look, I think he's almost ready to, um.... Can you wait for a second? Maybe over there." I pointed down the block. "Then I'll take him upstairs and come back down. If that's all right?"

"Terrific," he said, herding his dogs up the street.

"You'd better hurry, Buster," I muttered.

(*In the most delightful way.*)

XXX.

As I carted Buster upstairs to Mrs. Gudge, and ran back down to meet Petry, I commanded my brain to stop channeling *Mary Poppins*.

Then Petry and I, well, Petry and I and seven dogs, walked and talked. I managed to be totally in the moment for once, telling him about the Cheese Wheel and the video tape and Marcel's grab for me without a single *spoonful of sugar*.

Petry, for his part, got kind of stuck on Marcel's grabbing me. "What a frigging jerk," he kept saying. "What an a-hole. That must have been so horrible for you—"

"Yeah, it was awful," I said, even though a part of me felt suddenly absurdly happy about the whole thing. "But the point isn't the pass, it's the video. That's what Marcel was trying to hide, see? And the only reason he would have done that is to cover himself. Because the tape must show that you didn't do it. Which must mean…well, all I can think of is that maybe...Marcel stole the guitar? I mean, why else would he try so hard to pin it on someone else?"

"I still can't believe he grabbed you."

"Because you were in the Cheese Wheel, right? The night you lost your ID? Maybe it dropped out of your pocket there. Maybe Marcel found it. Maybe then *he* stole the guitar and planted your ID. Then made some switch of the video too."

"He must have really creeped you out,"

"Petry! Listen." I gently tugged one leash. (It was terrific, him being upset and protective, but we had to get past that.) "The guitar might still be there."

"In the store?"

"Seriously. There's this weird little closet, kind of a little cupboard, next to the counter that Marcel keeps locked. I almost opened it once, and you should have heard him freak."

"But why would he keep the guitar in the store where anyone could find it?"

We walked slowly, because we were thinking hard, but also because Charlie and Charcoal (Charcoal was one of the huge ones—a Borzoi, Charlie, a little brown and white King Charles) made a point of marking nearly every lamp post, hydrant, and trash can. That, in turn, seemed to inspire the female dogs, especially Sadie, an aging pug.

"That cupboard isn't open to just anyone," I said. "And maybe he didn't want to carry a guitar like that through the street."

"It would be in a case," Petry said.

"Maybe he didn't want it in his apartment."

"There's a thought. If he wasn't able to throw suspicion on me, he might have been a suspect. The police might even have searched his apartment. They came to ours."

I was quiet, thinking of what that must have been like, the police showing up at Petry's door, going through his stuff. It made me picture my own closet, crammed with my old clothes, Deanna's old clothes (things she'd gotten tired of that I still liked), Deanna's *new* clothes (things she couldn't wear that she had given to me—she tended to buy small), *Maddy's* old clothes, the papier mache cheetah I made in the third grade, half-empty bags of party loot, hidden vampire novels.

"And now Marcel's quitting. Which means we've got to act soon," I said urgently. "What if he leaves New York?"

"What do you mean, 'act'? What can we do?"

"Talk to your parents maybe?"

"I don't know if they'd listen," Petry sighed. "My mom would, but—" he reddened. "She and my dad are already fighting all the time about this. Hey, wait—this way—-" We stepped into the bright lobby of a big apartment building. "Charlie and Charcoal live here."

"Together?"

"Down the hall from each other." Petry pulled out a big ring of keys. "How about...I don't know...could you maybe talk to your friend?"

"Deanna?"

"Get her to have her dad check on Marcel?"

"We're kind of trying not to talk about all this stuff at the moment."

"Ah."

"And I'm not sure she'd believe me. She always kind of liked Marcel."

"She likes someone who accosted you?" Petry fumed.

"I didn't tell her about that. She probably wouldn't like him then."

Petry's eyes narrowed. "Creep."

Petry took back three dogs in that building, opening people's doors with his keys, walking into their kitchens, filling the dogs' water bowls with fresh water, locking the doors again.

It was odd being in strangers' apartments, tracking across their shag carpets, passing by their kitchen counters, not looking at their stacks of dirty dishes and laundry and mail—

"It's amazing how all these people just give you their keys and stuff."

"Especially since I'm a big thief," Petry said bitterly.

"They don't know about the charges?"

He looked at me. He did not say, "what do you think?" or anything snide like that, just shook his hair out of his face.

"I'm sorry," I whispered.

We came down the back stairs of the building and out at the corner of Jones Street and West 4th. And there at the far end of the block, so quiet, so glassy, so still (on the outside anyway), was the Cheese Wheel itself.

I could smell it from where we stood, like I had from Bleecker Street that afternoon—an odor of something rotten. And it wasn't just Limburger.

XXXI.

"How about…" I began, "how about we sneak in the store right now?"

"What do you mean?"

"Wait, no! I've got it! We sneak in, we hide, we wait till it closes, then we check out that little cupboard."

"After the store's closed?"

"Sure. Then, if we find the guitar, great. We call the police or Deanna's dad or take a picture of something. And if we don't find it, we let ourselves out and go home."

Petry was quiet.

"I know where the keys are," I said. "And I helped lock up the one day I worked. Besides, it's Friday. My mom won't care if I'm out late on a Friday."

"Yeah, but—"

"Seriously, Petry, we don't have much time. Not if Marcel's quitting soon. Once he quits—"

Petry bit his lip. "I guess we could just, you know, check it out," he said.

I pulled out my phone. It was only 5:45. Closing time wasn't till 7:30 on Fridays.

So what should we do? I didn't particularly want to wait on the street corner for an hour and a half, and also, well, my hair was filthy. (Not totally filthy, but it was getting that slightly slick feel that was okay for a Friday in school, but not a Friday night out.)

(Okay, we were planning on solving a crime, not going on a date, but it *was* Friday, it *would* be night, and we'd be *out*.)

"So, maybe we should just for split for a little while," I said, "and then meet up at about, I don't know, 7:10?" (Would that leave enough time for a blow dry?)

"You're going?" Petry asked, sounding almost upset.

My heart did a tiny flip.

"Just for a little bit."

"Oh, okay, yeah, sure," he sighed. "So, we'll meet back here then? At 7:10?"

"Cool."

"You know, Celia, you don't have to." Petry's voice lowered. "I mean, I absolutely want to meet up with you back here, but we don't have to go into the store."

My heart did a bigger flip. "We'll figure it out," I said.

As soon as I escaped Petry's range of vision, I ran. Down Bleecker, down Morton, then, once in my building, up the stairs.

I was meeting him at 7:10! And it was, what? Almost 6!

Thank God, it was Friday. Not just because it was, you know, *Friday*, but because this was one night my mom tended to come home a little later than usual.

I did *not* want to run into my mom. One look at my face and she was bound to sense something was off. Unless...I thought, jumping down to my bedroom floor—*yes!*

I couldn't quite make out the tune going on below—but the bass *bumdiddy* was absolutely clear.

I tore off my clothes, raced into the bathroom, turned on the faucet, jumped into the shower.

I tried to be quick, but I just had to let the gush of hot water and strawberrified herbs wash some calm over my head, my back, my shoulders.

As I attempted relaxation, snatches of song escaped my lips—

All I want is a room somewhere....

Somewhere...over the rainbow....

There were bells on the hill....

My Fair Lady, The Wizard of Oz, and *The Music Man* all in one lather cycle.

So much for relaxation.

Clothes weren't easy either. What do you wear when you want to look (a) official and crime-solvy; (b) sexy and (potentially) girl-friendy; and yet (c) ready, maybe, to hide in a closet.

The only thing I could come up with was mouthwash. And deodorant.

I finally decided on a slightly gathered skirt (cute and good for crouching) and my green hightops. (Black boots would be foxier but they made a lot more noise.)

The fact is that what Petry and I were setting out to do was technically illegal. Not just technically. It was so illegal that there was even a specific name for it—I couldn't remember that name just then, but I knew there was something. It was a crime that was probably even measured in degrees.

I purposely did not check my email. I did not want to hear from Deanna. I also was not in the mood to make excuses about weekend Pre-Cal homework, or to talk about how to handle Monday's test.

I finally towel dried my hair. Blow-drying would mean looking at myself in the mirror, and I was definitely not in the mood for a face-to-face with Hank.

Wrote a brief note to my mom—*"Out, maybe to a movie. Love—"*

That would keep her from wondering why my cell was off. Nice touch, Celia.

(Note to self: when you get to the Cheese Wheel, turn off cell.)

Got my coat, decided against a hat, even though my hair was still damp. Hats flattened and Hank did not do well with flat hair.

Locked the door.

Anyway, maybe Petry and I *would* end up at a movie.

As I rushed down the stairwell, I wished that I had gobbed on extra shampoo. My hair was clean enough, but I sure could have used more of those soothing herbs.

Lather, rinse, repeat.

Had I repeated?

XXXII.

(*Consider yourself at home!*)

I somehow made it down the stairs and out of my building with no broken bones. Thank God, part of my brain went.

Another part focused on *Oliver!*

(*Consider yourself part of the family!*)

The Artful Dodger! Now, there was a kid who knew how to get away with things.

(*We've taken to you so strong.*)

Anyway, Petry and I were not the thieves here—we were the thief-catchers.

(*It's clear we're going to get along.*)

Oops! Mom at the end of the block.

I did a full 180 and artfully dodged around the corner.

That's one great thing about New York City—you can almost always just zip down a different block or two and still end up at your chosen destination.

On Hudson Street now, I sprinted past the pizza parlor, giving a quick wave to the pizza guy who was cleaning off a table by the window. He waved back, seemingly not remembering how my mom and I had bugged him.

Got to the next corner, Barrow, parallel to Morton, hurtled up it.

(*Consider yourself well in.*)

The evening was a beautiful deep blue on Jones. Petry's cheekbones, under the street lamps, took on a purplish cast. Very nice, but he sure wasn't Brad, my treacherous brain said.

He smiled nervously, then "Marcel's not there," he whispered. "It's just that other guy."

My heart swelled with relief. I realized suddenly that I might not have been able to go back in the store with Marcel there. But Zach! Zach was a nice guy.

"Are you sure you want to go ahead with this?" Petry went on urgently. " I'm already in trouble." He pushed his hair out of his eyes. "But you don't have to be. You've already helped me plenty. Just to have you believe that I didn't do it is huge. I mean it, Celia. You don't have to prove anything."

In the warm glow that followed his words, my brain gushed into another song. From *Oliver!* again.

(*I'd do anything...for you dear...anything....*)

That's one that Nancy and Oliver sing—oh my gosh, he's so sweet (I'm talking about Oliver now)—in Fagin's attic.

"Come on, Petry. I *want* to help you. After all, you helped me."

"I helped you?"

"You know, with the basketballs."

"That was nothing."

"Saved me from summer school. Anyway, let's just see."

We stared at the brightly lit windows, peering around the special offer signs for Dutch Gouda, Irush Cheddar, Spanish Goats.

"Maybe we should just get a search warrant," Petry sighed.

The Maddy genes in me became instantly impatient. They wanted to tell him that it was only police who got search warrants. The Maddy genes wanted to declare that we shouldn't worry about getting into trouble, not if we were seeking the Truth. The Maddy genes wanted to say, look, if we want justice, we're going to have to make it ourselves, forget about the justice system. (Actually, I'm not sure about that last part. Maddy was always trying to start class action suits, so she probably did sort of believe in the justice system.)

I squelched all those genes. "It'll be okay," I said. "And if it's not, then we'll just leave."

"You promise?" Petry asked.

I nodded.

"So," Petry sighed. "How about if one of us tries to distract him, while the other goes to that little cupboard you were talking about?"

"It's not so easy to get behind the counter."

"But maybe we could just try. That way we could keep everything legal."

"Okay."

We went in together, but separately, if you know what I mean. Like two people who just happened to be walking in around the same time. Petry. aiming for unobtrusive, slipped instantly into the aisle farthest from the counter, disappearing among the Greek yogurts.

I had somehow forgotten about the cheese smell. I was not prepared for how it covered me like a thick sack inside the store itself. I had a hard time thinking clearly; I silently cursed Hank.

"Hey Celia!" Zach smiled as I slowly came up to the counter. "Long time no see. How goes it Bossfriend?" He winked.

It suddenly occurred to me that maybe we should just ask Zach about the guitar. About the little cupboard too.

But Zach could be involved in Marcel's scheming. Just because he *seemed* super-nice didn't meant that we could trust him.

Better stick to the plan.

(Errr...what plan?)

"I've been great," I said.

"Even without all the free cheese?" Zach laughed.

"Oh yeah." I tried to squelch the gag. "I sure have missed that! Um, but, seriously, I was wondering, um.... You didn't find anything?"

"Find anything?"

"Like a—a scarf," I invented. "I had this scarf from my grand-mother. It's—" I pictured Mrs. Gudge. "White with green and pink paisleys."

"Hmmm..." Zach scanned the space under the counter.

I stepped behind the counter too, wishing Petry and I had decided beforehand who was supposed to distract Zach and who was supposed to check out the little front cupboard.

As I pretended to look for my long lost scarf, I scanned the wall for the cupboard key.

"I'm afraid I just don't remember seeing it," Zach said, checking the shelves behind us. "White and green?"

"Yeah, and blue. I mean, pink." I had just found the place where the little cupboard key normally hung; it was gone.

"It was, um, my grandmother's too. I knew I shouldn't have worn it."

"You want to check out that storage closet in the back?"

163

"Sure thing," I said. "Hey, I can do it. You just stay put."

I found Petry behind the cookware.

"Watch out," he whispered, nodding at the hanging assortment of pastry cutters, spatulas, pie servers. "Some of those things are like knives. I was thinking that maybe one of them sliced my pocket—you know, the night my ID went missing."

He put a hand on my shoulder, I guess to shield it from the pastry cutters.

(*Would you climb a hill? Anything. Wear a daffodil? Anything.*)

"Did you see the key?" he asked. "To that little cupboard?"

I shook myself back into reality. "Nah, it's not there."

Petry sighed. "I thought it seemed too easy."

"But don't you see?" I whispered. "This is proof. I mean, if Marcel has Eric Clapton's guitar stuck in that cupboard, you think he'd leave the key right next to it? The fact that it's gone shows that Marcel probably really is hiding something."

"But if it's gone, what can we do?"

"Maybe we should try Plan B," I said.

"Plan B?"

"Hide in the storage closet till after the store's closed."

"I thought that was Plan A. *Actually*," Petry added reasonably, "I thought that plan was off the table."

"Ssshhh.... I'm supposed to be checking out the back closet. And you...you're not supposed to be here at all."

Acting braver than I felt, I opened the French doors of the storage closet. It was more crowded than I remembered.

Sshhh, I motioned, and nodded towards a space between the cartons.

Petry looked at me uncertainly.

I nodded again, harder.

Petry, still eyeing me, backed into the closet.

"I can't see it anywhere back here," I said loudly, shutting the doors and then walking back through the aisles to Zach.

Which is when I realized that now we'd only gotten *Petry* hidden.

"You're sure you left it here?" Zach asked, still looking into shelves.

"Um," I said, and "hmmm...."

Just then the store phone rang.

"Cheese Wheel," Zach picked up.

"Yes, this is an okay time. Store's slow." He winked at me again. "You want to know how the Swiss Emmentaler compares to the cave-aged Gruyere? And how the Danish Emmentaler fits in? And Jarlsberg? Besides being cheaper? How much do you think you might need?"

Zach picked up a price list. I gave him a smile, a wave, a shrug, all of which was supposed to mean that I'd given up on the scarf.

He smiled, waved, and shrugged back. I walked ostentatiously towards the door. When I saw that he was hunkered over the phone, I opened the door wide enough to make the bell ring, closed it, and scurried to the back storage closet. The French doors opened and Petry quickly quickly pulled me in.

XXXIII.

"Hey," Petry whispered, flattening his ribs against the boxes.

"Hey," I whispered back, flattening my ribs over a spurt of giggles.

"I got my brother to call."

"Harter?"

In the dim light, I could see the outline of Petry's face, his arm too. He raised it over my head and put it gently around my waist. I knew he was probably just putting his arm around me to make space— yes, because he was helping me off with my jacket now—still, it felt wonderful.

"Do you mind?" he whispered.

"Sshhh...." I whispered back.

He had taken off his jacket too. I could feel the warm softness of his forearm at my wrist.

"Hart will keep him busy for a while," he whispered.

"Can't they tell he's a kid?"

"Sure, but he's a kid they know. That guy, Zach, really digs him."

"Oh."

"He brings in a ton of business too. Gets my mom to come, the families of his friends—"

We both grew quiet, conscious that Zach's voice had hushed.

With the quiet arose a kind of panic. At least inside me. What if we couldn't find the cupboard key? What if we couldn't find the store key either? The one that would let us back out onto the street.

Even if we did find the key, even if we did get back out onto the street, how were we going to lock the door again so that the store wouldn't be robbed? And what about the metal gate?

I'd do anything, one part of my brain sang out.

Celia, you're an idiot, another part intoned.

"You want to sit down?" Petry whispered.

"I'm okay."

"If I squeeze into this box, bend my legs—"

"Ssshh."

I could hear the muted swishes of Zach's movements, footsteps. I kept my own body still, but on the inside, I was a mess. I had remembered the name for what we were doing—breaking and entering.

There wasn't any breaking involved—yet—but there was surely entering. And maybe we would cost Zach his job. And get Petry into even more trouble. Me too.

Just when I was ready for some serious hyperventilating, the lights dimmed. The bell that was attached to the outside door rang, followed by a metallic screech and a heavy jangle.

We waited a full five minutes. It felt like five hours. Petry, whose arm now held me close, ran a finger up and down my back. I tried to tell myself that there was something extremely romantic about being this close to a boy whose hair smelled good, even in a cheese store. I tried to wonder what kind of shampoo *he* used and whether it was calming and whether (the Maddy genes kicking in) it was tested on animals.

(*Would you lace my shoe? Anything!*)

All too soon the warmth of romance was damped by the chill of fear, as I focused on the fact that Petry and I were now locked into the store.

"What do you think?" he whispered.

"That we should go home."

He took his arm away. "Celia, I'm so sorry. Look, we can figure out the lock, or maybe call someone, maybe even the police; tell them that we made a mistake."

"No, come on." I sighed. "You brought a camera?"

"I've got one on my phone."

"Great."

Even though we were sure that Zach had gone, we opened the French doors of the back storage closet carefully. The store was absolutely still, the only light a pale reflection of the street. We tiptoed down the cookware aisle.

"Christ," Petry hissed, shaking his arm.

"What is it?"

"The blades on those things—" He pointed to a hanging bundle of pastry cutters.

"I'm amazed they aren't worried about getting sued." Petry went on, twisting his arm to see the back of it. His skin was as ghostly as a flashlight in the dim; the scrape showed dark and moist.

"Whoa. Those *are* sharp. Here, let me get you something to clean it."

I walked quickly behind the almost-familiar counter, immediately calmer with something human to tend to.

I pulled off a paper towel, wet it in a dribble of water, and took it back down the aisle to wipe down Petry's wrist. He held it out to me gratefully.

"You want me to look for some antiseptic?" I asked, as I pressed the towel against his skin. (There were fine, dark, slightly curled hairs there; they looked really nice and manly and....)

Petry stared at me with an expression that seemed almost pitying. "Let's just concentrate on the guitar, okay? And getting out of here."

"Sorry."

"So, there was a key?" Petry prompted.

"It used to hang on the wall. On that nail."

"Hmmm...."

"Wait, there was also a cup that had keys in it." I pulled out the big white mug with "Who's Boss?" on the side.

"Yes!!" I cried, shaking it.

"Fantastic!"

Just then, there were a couple of loud voices.

We ducked below the counter.

"12.99 for Irish Cheddar? They call that a special?"

"Nah, that's a good deal. They got great stuff at this place."

Passersby. Outside. Already gone. Still, they'd put a serious cramp in my euphoria.

"It's this little cupboard, right?" Petry prompted again, bending down by the wall.

"I always thought it looked like an elves' closet," I whispered, then almost bit my tongue. (*Elves' closet?!*)

"It does sort of look like that," Petry mused, twisting the locked handle.

I handed him the cup.

There were a lot of keys in it. They made me realize (all over again) that I hadn't worked at the shop long enough to really understand anything about its keys.

Petry poured the keys onto the floor, quickly scanning them for likely prospects.

His face did not look as if he'd found any. Still, he began trying them. "Could there be more someplace else?"

I searched the main counter area, reaching into all the nooks, crannies, another couple of mugs. One had an old tea bag in it, eeuw, only half desiccated.

Petry kept trying out the keys from the floor even though those left looked like they couldn't possibly fit. "If you were hiding the extra key to a little elves' closet," he whispered, half to himself, "where would you put it?"

"If I were Marcel you mean," I groaned, running my hands through my hair.

Then I knew. I reached down for the small coffee can of hair nets that sat on a shelf below one of the cutting boards. In the semi-darkness of the shop, the hair nets looked like a cloud of mouse dreams. I totally hate anything having to do with mice, but made myself stick in one hand.

Just under the tangled bunch of netting was something small, flat, cold, jagged, and almost too light to be made of metal.

Almost.

XXXV.

Petry took the key silently, pushed it into the lock, and turned. It made a wonderful chunky click.

"Open Sesame," he whispered.

I had imagined that the guitar would sit there shimmering, its strings sounding a spontaneous ta-da.

But all I saw were boxes. In the light from the street, I could barely make out the words printed on the sides: "Biscuits de L'Huile d'Olive."

"Not more crackers!"

"Wait a minute," Petry said. Threading himself between boxes and the closet wall, he slowly pulled out a long black oblong case.

"But that's not even shaped like a guitar."

"It's an electric. Hey!" Petry reached into the closet again. "I think there's a couple of others."

Petry pulled two more guitars from the space between the boxes. I helped him lift them out to the floor.

I lay the first one down on its side and opened its case.

It didn't actually go ta-da, but it was still amazing—all shimmery and gold and metallic brilliant blue.

"Is that the Clapton?"

Petry didn't say anything, just opened the next one, and the next, and, actually, they were all shiver-worthy. The second was black and silver, the third shades of red—all beautiful and sleek and shiny, all radiating silent but incredibly cool guitar riffs.

"Wow." Petry's mouth hung slightly open.

"Which is it?"

"I'm trying to think of what Clapton is known for," Petry said. "They're all Stratocasters, all classics too."

Just outside came an insistent rattle of metal. This was not a passerby.

We instantly (as instantly as we could) flipped the cases shut.

The gate over the outside door slid open with metallic skid. Petry pushed the cases back behind the cracker boxes. He bent down to get into the cupboard too, taking my hand, pulling me along.

"Petry, no! We won't be able to fit," I pulled back.

"To the other one then."

There wasn't time to lock the elf door. We just swooshed around the counter, through the aisles, back towards the rear storage closet. In the last aisle, the one where Petry had cut himself, a pleat in my gathered skirt caught on a slotted spatula, hooking me to a display.

"Petry!"

A key turned, the bell tinkled. Petry, holding his breath, unhooked the spatula from the display, carrying it behind me as we both slipped into the storage closet. I pulled the French doors shut behind us.

I shut my eyes too, trying to tell myself to keep cool. But it was hard to keep cool with someone padding around the shop, singing what sounded, in the distance, like *"La Vie en Rose."*

I wanted to say to Petry, 'maybe he'll just check the cash register, then leave.' As if saying that could make it happen.

I wanted to ask, 'did we pick up the keys from the floor?' As if asking could make that happen.

What I really wanted was to scream.

Petry just looked at me, his face so close in the darkness that I felt a whole new rush of excitement, nervousness, warmth—

(*I'd do anything for—*)

A loud snapping noise jerked my mind back into the storage closet, my terrified crazy mind.

I looked into Petry's face again, and, in the dim, saw his lips moving. Was he also singing inside? Or was it prayer?

I tried some. *Dear God, I know you've got more important things to be concerned about, all those droughts, etc., but please please please just let him be stopping by for some cheese.*

The crack in between the two French doors of our closet lit up and something sounding like a French curse seeped in.

I froze. Icier. My heart, which I thought had already stopped beating, truly stopped.

But the light switch was in the front of the store, I told myself. But it was a distant curse. But he wasn't actually in our aisle, was he?

And then he was.

The French doors slammed open.

Marcel's face was screwed up in both fury and irritation. And he held, in one low hand, something small and silvery that did not shimmer, and yet somehow drew the eye.

"Come out slowly," he hissed, "wiz zee hands over zee head."

XXXVI.

I almost started to laugh. "Wiz zee hands over zee head" sounded like a villain in a cartoon.

Then I realized that the small, silvery, non-shimmering thing was a gun. It was small enough to be a toy gun, but it had a darkness at the center of its barrel that did not belong to a toy.

"I can explain," Petry started.

Marcel slapped him with his gun hand. Petry's head whipped to the side.

A terrible high pitched cry wailed around us. Marcel glared at me. "Shut it, you."

Petry doubled over, grunting like he was sick, his hand to the side of his mouth. I moved to help him, but Marcel stuck his gun arm between us, pushing us apart.

"Stop it," I cried. "Leave us alone."

"Ahh, it is the little girl who didn't like so much zee Cheese Wheel. Yet she comes back for more. Why is zis do you suppose?"

Petry spoke huskily. "We'll go. Call the cops if you want." He took his phone out of his pocket. It turned bright as he flipped it open.

Before Petry's thumb could dial 911, Marcel hit the phone out of his hand. It went flying into the aisle of pots and pans, hitting something that half-heartedly reverberated, then clunked heavily onto the floor.

"None of zat, boy. You break into my shop, you can't call zee police on me."

"He wasn't calling the police on you," I babbled. "He was turning himself in, turning us in, I mean. It was wrong for us to come here, a silly prank; we thought we'd be alone, sample some cheeses. I really love those crackers you have, you know the olive oil ones. And the chocolate, yum—"

"Zee chocolate tastes sickeningly of cheese. You know zat, I know zat. You didn't break in for zee chocolate."

"But I like cheesy chocolate," I babbled. "I have this friend—actually, you know her. Deanna, Mr. Z's daughter, with the super spiky red hair, only it's purple right now, or pink, I don't know. Anyway, she always makes hot chocolate and then dips cheese and bread in it."

Marcel looked at me like I was crazy; even Petry, still holding his mouth, looked at me like I was crazy.

"Well, she does."

"Hah!" Marcel said. "But me, I am not interested in zee chocolate. I am interested in zee *guitars*." He waved the gun towards Petry. "You are him, right? The boy who lose his ID. The boy who steal the guitars."

"He didn't steal any guitars." I blurted out.

"What about the ones he pull from my cupboard just tonight?"

Petry pressed a leg against mine in warning, then turned a bewildered face to Marcel. "Huh?"

Marcel swung the gun towards Petry's face again.

This time, I didn't scream. I jumped onto Marcel's arm, holding on tight, hoping to give Petry time to do something.

This tactic might have worked if Petry was not being pistol whipped onto the floor. (I had probably blocked the full force of the blow, but I had not been able to stop it.)

As a result, it was me against Marcel and Marcel was a thickly built, strong man, who was also, it seemed, ambidextrous. Before I even understood what he was doing, he had twisted my arms behind my back, kicked out my kicking legs, and pressed something cold and circular into my no-longer-swallowing throat.

I did not babble now. I did not cry out. I didn't even think of breathing. All around me was the horrible odor that Marcel's body exuded, an odor of winey, rennety, sweaty, tobacco-y, cheese.

There was no question of gagging. There was no room for a bulge in my esophagus with the gun muzzle pressed there.

"Boy," he said, nodding at Petry. "I want you to walk down zee aisle, yes, just ahead of me. Don't do anyzing silly, eh? Or I shoot. I have the great excuse for shooting, eh—you two break in my shop— and, you know, I don't even need such a good excuse right now."

Petry slowly got up from the floor. "You can't shoot two unarmed kids," he croaked. "The police won't buy that."

"Just go—" Marcel said, kicking him in the side.

"It's not worth it," Petry insisted. "Grand larceny's one thing, but agg assault—"

"Move, boy." Marcel leaned forward to give Petry a hard shove. I heard a loud ripping sound. "*Merde*," Marcel hissed. As he craned to look at his backside, he pressed the gun barrel deeper into my throat. "I told that Zach we must fix zese pastry cutters. Zey'll get us sued." He laughed as if this was all one big joke.

In the midst of his laughter, I prayed for Petry to do something. I prayed for myself to do something. Okay, I didn't want Marcel to shoot me, but I kept thinking of what my mom always said about people trying to force you into a car. Do anything rather than get in, she always said. Even if they've got a gun.

My panicking mind hooked onto that word—*anything*.

(*I'll do anything....*)

Only now it remembered the dark side of the song—when Fagin sings, Fagin, the old fence who turns all the little boys into pickpockets: *would you rob a shop? Anything. Even risk the drop? Anything. Till your eyes go pop?*

My popping eyes stared at the back of Petry's head as he slowly, hands-up, walked down the aisle. I felt like I could see his brain darting through options even through the disheveled locks of hair, even through his skull. Would he pull down the rack of cookware? Would I be able to get out of the way?

I could almost feel the pots and pans raining down—a slow blur of copper-bottomed motion—when Marcel said, "Hold on zere boy." The next moment, Marcel, taking the gun from my throat, hit Petry on the back of the head.

Petry's body crumpled; I screamed.

Marcel clapped his hand over my mouth, yanked my hair, thrust the gun deep into my side.

"One I can handle," he whispered. "But two—it eez much, even for me, zee big cheese." He laughed. Dragging me over Petry's clumped form, he pulled me down the aisle.

I should have bit harder. I should have kicked harder. *I* should have grabbed at the cookware. When I replayed the scene in my mind later, I could think of a zillion and one things that might have worked.

But at that moment, nothing seemed possible. Even my throat was on lock-down.

He pushed me to the door that led down to the basement. With his gun hand, he fiddled with the lock. After leaning in to turn on the light, he shoved me into the narrow stairwell.

This shook me from my paralysis, the basement like that car my mother warned against.

I pulled, I twisted, I bit. When Marcel moved his hand from my teeth, I started screaming again. He let go, but only to curse and then push me. I fell down the metal stairs, twisting and crashing, something sharp gouging my thigh.

I put one arm out to catch myself, the other over my face. This meant that when I landed, which seemed to happen again and again, my forearms and elbows, knees, thighs, and one ankle were jabbed with pain, while my nose and eyelids seemed hardly bruised.

But I didn't have time to figure out what hurt. Marcel was dragging me to a heavy set of shelves against the opposite wall. Like the other shelves, it was stacked with huge round cheeses, waxy moons of red and orange that seemed stupidly serene in the middle of my star-shooting haze.

"Zere," he growled, his weight forcing me into the frigid cement.

"Please," I whimpered. "You don't want to do this. I'm...having my period. It's really heavy, and seriously—"

"I'm not going to attack you, you stupid girl." He kneed me into the floor, forcing me to a spot next to the shelf. "You *want* I should attack you?"

"Help," I screamed. "Help!"

"Shut it," Marcel hissed, pulling one of my own arms over my face. "Shut the mouth now, or I make you."

Maybe it was stupid—it was probably stupid—but I shut.

He had put the gun down. I could see its dull glint from the floor as I turned my face to the side, but there was no way I could make a grab for it. He held both my arms tightly, pulling my hands together, and his full weight pressed me down, flattening my breasts. I did not really have my period, but I *was* having PMS, which, as he forced my breasts into the icy cement, got about a billion times more intense.

"Please," I whimpered.

As he coiled thick packing twine around and around my wrists, arms, and legs, my throbbing brain slid senselessly back to *Oliver! (I'd do anything for you, dear, anything.)*

"Turn over," he said.

I tightened my body into a hard, resisting plank.

He took hold of my shirt, pulling and twisting me closer to the large shelves. He pushed the twine into the back of one shelf, squeezing it behind and under the shelves, winding and winding. Every few winds, he tested the twine, then tightened. "You pull this out—bam!" he warned. "You will wish zat you hadn't."

He picked up his gun. "Keep your mouth shut or I hurt the boy. No blague." Then he clattered back up the stairs.

I was so freaked out by this time that I almost cried out 'don't go,' though of course, I wanted him to go. At least, I didn't want him near me. Still, there was something terrible about being left, tied up, in that basement—it was a cellar really—even with the lights on, even with its bright white walls.

Marcel was down again soon enough, carrying Petry by arms and head, dragging his feet behind.

I could see him bending over Petry then, tying him up too. Petry did not seem to be exactly conscious, though I could hear occasional moans.

I moaned back.

"Sshh," Marcel hissed. "You want I hit him again?"

"Help!" Petry called out suddenly, his voice scratched, feeble.

Marcel shook him. "Shut it. You want I hurt *her* again?"

Petry was quiet then too.

"Zat door," Marcel motioned towards a cellar door that seemed to be at the top of some kind of small conveyor belt, a delivery door that, I figured, opened onto the sidewalk. "It is among zee heaviest made. Mr. Z., he don't like zee stealing of cheese. Not by people, not by rats. Zere are no cracks here. No holes, no little crevasse. Well, maybe zee littlest of holes. I have seen a mouse to be sure—they get in a hole no bigger than a dime, and the cucurachas—even less than that. Even zose big ones."

I felt things crawling around my legs. It felt almost worse than the aches, worse even than the burning of the twine, the stinging cold of the cement.

I remembered how I had once imagined the Cheese Wheel as a backdrop for a musical comedy number, and my dazed brain began to laugh weakly. Characters in Broadway musicals suffer, sure—bad things happen. But there's not a single musical I can think of in which cockroaches happen.

Marcel bent down to check my twine once more.

"C'est bon." He walked back across the room to squat beside Petry. He seemed to have tied him to a whole metal shelving system. He tugged at the twine on his legs, making sure it was secure.

"Alors," he said. "Je reviens. Don't think about making zee noise, eh? I will be just upstairs."

Then, suddenly, after everything going so completely dismally wrong, something good happened.

Marcel stopped to stretch—first a loose, grunting straddle, then he leaned against a wall, arching his back. As he spread his legs, the tear in his back pocket widened; from that gap slipped a small silvery object.

The gun?

I squinched up my eyes. No. He still held the gun in one hand. There it was, outlined against the wall he leaned into.

A green light blinked as the silvery object slid along some leaves of cardboard laid out on the floor, then slipped silently into their folds.

A cell phone.

Marcel straightened, lightly shaking his arms. I waited for him to bend down and look for the phone in the folds of cardboard. Instead, he waved the gun towards me, "Ciao for now, eh," and clambered back up the stairs.

When he reached the top, he flicked the light switch—off, then on, then off again.

I heard the shutting of the door next, the sliding of a deadbolt.

XXXVII.

It was not the kind of darkness you normally see in the city, which is no darkness at all. There is always some kind of light—a street lamp, store window, car, neon sign, a checkerboard of fluorescence in an office building, a TV screen in an apartment. Sometimes, when you look up, you'll even see the blue glow of someone's aquarium.

In the city, it's never even dark inside—there's always something—your computer monitor, the cable box, the bright little circle on the smoke detector, the aura of the street sneaking between the blinds. Even though Maddy insisted we turn everything off in order to save CO_2 emissions, there was always some small glow.

Not like here.

"Celia." Petry's whisper was hoarse. "Are you okay?"

"I don't like this."

"No," he whispered. "Me neither."

"Petry, are *you* okay? He hit you really hard."

He sighed. "Whatever wisdom teeth I might be growing are going to be seriously impacted."

"I'm sorry," I moaned.

"*You're* sorry? I'm the one who should be sorry. You were just trying to help."

"Yes, but I should have thought things through better. At least told my mom what we were doing. Well, I probably couldn't have told her, but I could have told my sister. She'd understand. She wanted to break into some nuclear warhead facilities."

"I could have told Harter. I guess I didn't want to seem like a bad influence, like my dad's been saying."

"You're not a bad influence."

"I may not be any influence at all pretty soon."

Faint sounds vibrated overhead.

"What do you think he's doing up there?"

I could feel Petry listening.

I could feel myself listening.

"Talking to somebody?" he whispered.

"But who?"

"On the phone?"

"Oh Petry, I forgot to tell you. Marcel dropped his cell. When he was stretching."

"Where?"

"Over there. I mean, towards your…um…right. In the packing boxes."

"He didn't pick it up? "

"I don't think so. I don't think he noticed it. Mine is in my jacket. In the stupid closet upstairs. And yours—"

"Yeah, I know. Probably smashed."

"But, maybe we could—" I tugged at my unmoving shelf. "Oh crap—you think he'll come back for it?"

"I think we better find it before he does."

The faint murmur of talk overhead was interrupted by a huge thudding crash from Petry's direction, followed by a bunch of smaller thuds.

"Petry!"

"Petry," I cried again.

"What are those big round ones? Goudas?" he panted.

"Are you okay?"

"I've been better. Where did you say the phone was?"

"It was to your right, by the wall, mixed into the pieces of cardboard."

I could feel the rush of movement again, hear metal scraping against the floor.

"Are you still attached to the shelf?"

"I think so."

"You *think* so?"

"I'm pretty sure something big is following me, and I don't think it's Marcel."

"Petry, what if he heard?"

We hushed.

The murmur upstairs continued.

"Wait—you hear that? Daaa da dunda. It sounds like what they play for the traffic report. You know, on the radio."

I felt the air lurch, and then what seemed to be Petry's head sank onto my outstretched legs.

"Ouch," he said.

It was his head all right. Through the rips in my tights, I could feel the softness of his lips, the bend of his nose. "Are you okay?"

"It's your knees," he whispered.

"I'm sorry if they're knobbly," I whispered, feeling an insane gush of happiness. "Yours are too."

"Nice knees." He turned his face onto its side, his ragged breathing slowly settling.

It was so strange to have his head on my legs—wonderful, but in the midst of the cold and fear—strange.

And quiet. Too quiet.

I jiggled my knees. "Petry! You're not going to sleep on me?"

He moved his head groggily. "I'm just trying to think which way is right. You said, right, right? I'm not coming up with it."

"Wait a second. If it's the radio playing, that may mean Marcel's not upstairs. And if he's not upstairs, maybe we can just *shout* for help. Maybe you don't have to crawl all over the place."

"If he hears us, he'll come down."

"But if he's gone—"

We listened. In the midst of the murmur was a jingle of music, the kind used for commercials.

"It really does sound like the radio," Petry said.

"Yeah," I whispered. But when I thought about shouting for help, the outline of the silver gun filled my throat.

Then, in the stillness, something fast, furry and possibly toe-nailed skimmed by a tear in my stocking. My scream was instant and very very loud.

"Celia!" Petry's head shot up in the darkness.

"I'm sorry. It was just a ...m...m...mouse. Maybe. So stupid."

Petry laughed gently. "That's one mouse that won't come out again any time soon. Wait—"

I listened. "It's the same, right?"

"There's no way he could miss that scream."

"You're right," I whispered. "Petry, you're right. Help," I tried shouting. "Help."

"Help," Petry groaned.

We stopped, listened again. There was only the thick hum of refrigeration, and above that, the hushed murmur of what we hoped was the radio.

"What's wrong with people?"

"It's Friday night. In the Village. Halloween coming. That door also looks pretty thick."

"Heelllpp!" I sang it this time; my voice hurt too much to shout.

"Hey, that's good. You get a lot of volume like that."

"Heelllppp!" I sang again.

"You've got a great voice, you know."

"Thanks."

Yes, it was ridiculous. Here I was tied up to a shelving system of goudas in a cold basement, threatened by a homicidal maniac. And a mouse. And possible cockroaches. And yet my heart was soaring just because some guy complimented my singing voice.

But he was a really sweet guy, who was being way too quiet again.

"Petry."

"Ummm."

"Please don't fall asleep."

"Huh...."

"I mean, you might have a concussion, right? And we've got to get to that phone. Listen, what can I do?"

"Wait," he whispered. "To the—what did you say? The right?" He started to worm forward.

"Petry, you're climbing up *me* now."

"I know," he panted. "But if I can free you, then we can both go."

"Okay but be careful. These shelves are really heavy."

Petry leaned back for a moment. In the next, his face was nuzzling my neck.

"Petry...um...."

"I'm trying to bite the twine."

I tried to laugh. I tried not to laugh. I tried to think of Marcel coming back. I tried not to think of Marcel coming back.

"Wait, Petry. Stop. Maybe you could use the spatula."

"Huh?"

"You know, the one on my skirt. It's still stuck there. You'll have to hold it in your mouth though. And then, um, maybe go for the stuff near my waist. I think that's where I'm tied to the shelves."

"Ah."

Petry wormed his way down my torso, then nosed my skirt. (Yes, it felt weird.) "'Ot it,'" he whispered.

"Will it reach the twine?"

"I'll 'af to 'ull it off your 'irt."

His head weaved back and forth over my thighs as he tried to loosen the slats of the spatula. I arched, lifting my bum off the floor. Finally, with a really determined pull, he wrested it away.

And now I could feel the sharp edge of the spatula at my waist. I moved my torso as much as I could so that I was sawing from the other direction.

For a long time, it seemed like we weren't getting anywhere. Then, suddenly, the twine loosened, frayed, snapped—and I was free.

Of the shelves.

XXXVII.

"'ou 'ant —'e to 'o your 'ands and 'eet?"

"Sure."

I rolled over. Petry pushed himself against me, trying in the darkness to wedge the blade between my wrists this time, to get at the stuff that bound them together.

But after a minute, he dropped the spatula, panting. "He's used so much of that crap."

"Maybe we better just get to the phone."

"Look, you have to kind of propel yourself, right?" Petry said. "But when you do, watch out for *my* shelf. It's just behind me somewhere."

"Okay."

"There's a bunch of those big cheeses too."

"I swear I'm never going to eat cheese—"

Petry tried to laugh: it came out as a gasp.

"Petry!"

"I'm just—" He breathed.

"I'll go first. You take a little break, okay?"

"Watch out for my shelf," he warned again.

Ouch.

I started again, this time more carefully.

It was very difficult to move with hands and feet tied. I felt like fish on dry land. Actually, a fish in a dry parking lot. With speed bumps.

"Remember the cheeses."

"I'm learning about the cheeses."

Just then I heard a snuffling noise and the drag of metal.

"I thought you were taking a breather."

"You might need help."

"You should rest your head."

"My head was never my strong point."

Petry was quite good at lunging across the floor, even tied to the shelf.

"Watch out for me," I cried out just in time.

A face met mine.

"You know how I can tell it's you?" Petry whispered.

"Because I'm the only other person down here?"

"No," he chuckled. "It's your nose. I can tell by your nose."

I groaned.

"Hey, I love your nose," Petry protested.

"Stop."

"I mean it. You have a truly magnificent nose."

"Let's just look for the phone, okay?"

"Have you noticed how many wonderful singers have them?" Petry gasped as we lunged on.

"What?"

"Big noses."

"Please. I am so sick of hearing about Barbra Streisand."

"Maria Callas, Beverly Sills, Nathalie Dessay—"

"But they all do opera, right?"

"Joan Baez. Patti Lupone. Patti Smith. Bob Dylan. John Lennon"

"The last two are men. And Bob Dylan's not really a great singer."

"Try to beat him."

"You know what I mean."

"Okay, so there's...uh...Aretha Franklin, Julie Andrews."

"Aretha's nose is nice."

"Nice, not teeny."

"And Julie Andrews has a cute little nose."

"Cute, but not particularly little. I think it has something to do with resonance. Nasal resonance."

"Wait, here's some cardboard." I nosed a piece up. "And there! See the green light."

Petry flung himself towards it. I could see his hair flapping in the sporadic glow; I also caught a glint of tooth. Was he going to pick the phone up in his mouth? I tried not to think of Marcel palming the stupid thing with his cheesy tobacco-ey fingers.

The word 'resonance' popped into my mind—cheesy resonance, sweaty resonance—when what I wanted to think about was nasal resonance. Whatever it was that Petry meant. You couldn't need a big nose to be a good singer.

"I hate to pick it up with my mouth," Petry said. "It's kind of sore, and...uh...I keep thinking of the gun."

I could feel his shudder. "I'll do it."

"Oh Christ, no," he said. "After all this I'm bound to be getting a tetanus shot, what do you think?"

I gasped. The dim light of the phone shone more directly on him now that he had it between his teeth.

"Petry—your face—"

He spat out the phone. "We've got to flip it open, right?" He tried to do something with his chin. It looked completely misshapen in the green light.

"Let me." I nuzzled the phone from Petry. Then, there was just no choice. This was a job for Hank.

But it was hard. It seemed to take forever to get Hank's tip positioned under the phone's lid. I just about had it when the phone started to slip away. Luckily, it was caught by Petry's swollen jaw.

"Once more," he whispered.

This time I stuck Hank up in the air, trying to think of all the people I felt snooty towards—Brad, the STC, Tracy, Jessica, Emma, even Deanna, Deanna with a part in the musical. Then dove Hank down to catch the lid.

"Amazing," Petry whispered. "Can you dial 911?"

I took aim, then dove Hank down again.

A whole host of numbers started up.

"Damn. I got a speed dial."

A woman's voice answered. "Wash Your Mouth Out Phone Service at your service. The credit card on file with this number will be charged $8 for the first three minutes—"

"You want to try again?" Petry asked. "You want me to try?"

"No, wait—I know this number."

"Hey, Big Boy," came a breathy voice. "Looking for something hot and juicy—"

"You *know* that number?"

I scanned my memory for names. "Is this Louise?"

"Louise? No, honey, this is Selma."

Selma, oh yes. Selma who had walked while she talked because she wanted to lose some weight. Selma who had cooed at my back.

"Selma, do you remember me? I worked there one night? For Soft Soap and the warranty stuff? The girl with the brown hair who sat in front of you?" I lowered my voice, looking away from Petry. "The one who Larry called 'Nosey?'"

"Wait a second. You that girl that run out?"

"That's right. Listen, Selma, I'm in a tight spot. I've been tied up by this really awful guy in a cellar; so could please you call 911?"

"This a joke, honey? You seemed like a nice kid, but Larry, he won't want us calling the police."

"Selma, please." Tears came to my eyes. "I'm tied up in the basement of a store on Jones Street, the Cheese Wheel. I don't know the exact address but it's Jones off Bleecker, you know, in the West Village. I'd call the police myself, but I can't. Seriously. I just got you by accident on this crazy guy's phone. I was dialing with my nose."

"She's telling the truth," Petry croaked.

"Wait a second. You the crazy guy tying her up?"

"No, not him," I interjected. "Look, if you don't want to call the police, then call my mom—actually, could you please call her right now anyway, and tell her it's Celia and I'm at the Cheese Wheel and she needs to get the police right away."

"You want me to call your mom? And tell *her* to call the police."

"I'll pay you."

"Me too," Petry said.

"Naw, you don't have to pay me. Why don't you just, you know, stay on the line—you got someone else's phone right? Just let the call stretch out a little while I call your mom. Now, what's your name again?"

"Celia."

"And your number?"

I told her. Then we were put on hold. A tape played: *"ooh baby, hold on tight."*

Petry's eyes widened (at least the eye that wasn't swollen shut).

"You worked at that place?"

"Only for one night. That's when I called you that first time."

We were head to head now. It might have been nice, except for all the moans in the background.

"I hope she gets through," I whispered.

"She will," Petry whispered back.

After forever and a half, "Celia," Selma said. "You still there?"

"I'm here."

"Man, your mom's upset. I told her I'd call 911, I don't care what Larry says, but she said she's calling it herself. *And* she's on her way. She said I should call your number too, boy, your folks. So what's *your* name?"

"Petry."

"Never heard of that one. Short for Peter or something?"

"Something," Petry said.

"Petry," I hissed.

"Actually, it's a combination of Peter and Harry," he sighed. "My parents couldn't make up their minds."

"Can be pretty hard sometimes, two people having to agree," Selma said. "What's your number?"

He gave it to her.

"You kids just hold on tight now."

"A combination of Peter and Harry," I said quietly. "That's kind of nice."

"Better than Harter."

The tape moaned again, *"oh baby, hold on tight."* I tried to pretend it was just another song in my head, a not very good song.

"You don't think Marcel will come back?" I wondered suddenly.

"The police should be here soon."

"Yes, but—maybe we should—I don't know—hide."

"In the dark?"

"We could at least try to undo our hands. Mine seem a little looser."

"I left the spatula by the cupboard."

"Maybe, if we go back to back, I could use my fingers to work on yours and you could work on mine."

"Okay."

We wriggled around like the hands of a broken clock.

"There," he sighed.

"Petry," I laughed. "We're still front to front. Almost exactly like we were."

"Oh. Oh yeah."

And now, as the *"babies"* oohed around us, Petry's face leaned into mine.

He moved so slowly I thought he might be conking out again.

He wasn't.

He kissed me one, two, three, four times. Each time seemed slower, deeper than the last; each time his lips felt softer, warmer, more and more amazing.

The only bad part—and it wasn't exactly bad—was that they tasted faintly of blood.

But I didn't think about that much after the second kiss. All I could think of was how frustrating it was that we couldn't touch each other, our hands still tied behind our backs.

Except that after the third kiss, even being tied up was kind of wonderful. Not having my hands loose seemed to make me feel *exactly* where his shoulders bent into my shoulders; *exactly* where his chest pressed into my chest; *exactly* where one of his tied-up thighs pressed against one of my tied-up thighs. Every place our bodies touched overwhelmed the stinging, the hurt, the cold. It felt as if absolutely nothing in the world could come between us and what we needed to do just then.

(*Some enchanted evening…you may see a stranger…you may see a stranger across a crowded room—*)

Of course, Petry wasn't a stranger, I could hardly see him in the darkness, and the only thing that crowded this room was fallen cheeses. Still, the song seemed right.

Until sirens whined overhead. So much for *Some Enchanted Evening*. Our bodies jerked apart. Even the *"ooh babies"* cut off.

"Hey you, Peter Harry," came Selma's voice. "Your dad's a real pain. But he's on his way."

"Selma, thank you so much."

"Yeah," Petry whispered, "yeah, thanks."

There were reverberations on the sidewalk overhead: heavy investigatory feet. We both began calling for help.

"Sing it," Petry rasped.

Though I felt silly, I did as he asked—I really did get a lot of volume that way.

A crash, and now someone banged on the floor just exactly over our heads. My heart flooded with every kind of good feeling—that had to be my mom. She was the only person who, hearing my sung 'helps', could have sited us with such absolute precision.

"We're down here," I cried.

It took a couple of minutes, and another couple of crashes. I wondered whether maybe we should have called Mr. Z for the keys.

Then five policemen and my mom were beside us. Less than a minute later, red-faced, and breathing as if he'd just sprinted eight blocks, was a man who looked for all the world like he must be Petry's dad.

One of the policemen had a big flashlight, which he waved in my eyes, until another policeman cursing, ran back up the stairs and flicked the switch by the door.

In the blinking brilliance all I could make out were dark blue pants, black shoes, and my mom's 'darling's.'

Sometimes moms can be embarrassing. This was not one of those times. There is nothing like being tied hand and foot on a cellar floor and surrounded by the legs of policemen for making you feel vulnerable. Especially when you have just been kissing a boy who is still only about two inches away, has longish lankyish hair, and was arrested the previous week.

As my mom hugged, a policeman cut the twine on my wrists and feet. I could hardly shake them they hurt so much; I couldn't stand up either. My mom started rubbing with a vengeance.

In the light, Petry's face showed a bruise forming over one very swollen eye and a dark purple blotch on the side of his jaw and cheek.

"Petry, Jesus," his dad cried, kneeling beside him. "Look at his face, officer. Son, what happened to you?"

'Oh—uh—" Petry tried.

"We found out who took the guitar," I said. "It was Marcel, the guy who works here."

"You found out who took the guitar?" Petry's dad said.

"He was the guy that tied us up. And hit Petry. With a gun. I mean, Petry was amazing."

"She was the one who was amazing," Petry said, his one clear eye looking my way.

A very large police officer, whose knees squeaked as he squatted next to us, flipped open a little notepad. "Okay kids, so tell me all about it."

XXXVIII.

Petry did have a concussion, though it wasn't a bad one, the doctors said. X-rays had to be taken of my ankle and his face (nothing fractured, thankfully), and there was a huge amount of paperwork. One policeman sat next to us in the emergency room, jotting things down. This was actually not so bad since (a) the policeman, Officer Mahoney, was totally impressed that we had been trying to save Eric Clapton's guitar, and (b) it meant that the hospital people didn't make us wait quite so long. It also meant that they had to keep Petry and me together in the same little curtained-off booth while people in white uniforms poked us and shone little flashlights in our eyes. Some time in the middle of it all, Petry's dad got a call that Marcel had been apprehended at Kennedy Airport with three stolen guitars, as well as a small suitcase of cash and about fifty jars of caviar (wadded inside some berets.)

"Yes!" my mother said.

"Looks good for you, son," Petry's dad said, rubbing Petry's arm.

I felt like saying that it always looked good for Petry, since he had never done anything wrong, but I didn't want to upset Petry's father.

He'd been great with the police and the hospital people, and with Petry too.

Now, he turned to me.

"I want to thank you, Celia, from the bottom of my heart. I'm not saying that what you two did was right," he sighed. "There had to have been a less risky way to go about this. But I really do appreciate your trust in my son and I'm sorry for being short with you on the phone the other day. I'm sorry to you too, son," he turned to Petry. "It was wrong of me not to trust you, absolutely wrong."

Just about then Petry's mother and brother came sneaking through the curtain. His mother was a pretty woman with Petry's eyes and smile.

"Oh darling," she cried, throwing her arms around Petry. Tears streamed down her face. Petry's dad stretched an arm around both of them.

Little Harter chimed in from the foot of the bed. "Yo bro! They said only one person to a patient until I gave them all the chocolates I made."

"You!" Petry whispered around his mom's hug, pointing one finger at his brother.

"I managed to save one though." Harter squeezed by the hospital bed and brought out a Tupperware container that held one small round of dark chocolate. It looked almost exactly like a chocolate from a fancy chocolate store except that it had a strange light brown blotch on its top.

"Give it to them." Petry nodded toward my mom and me.

"No," I protested.

"Please," Harter said.

"Yes, please, do try it," Petry's mom said.

"They're very good," Petry's dad said,

Harter's round face reddened with pride. "That light brown stuff is caramel," he said, pointing to the chocolate's top. "I'm trying to use it for decorating."

"Sounds great," my mom said.

"And that shape is supposed to be an elephant, but I'm really really bad at them."

Petry cuffed him gently in the arm. "Well, I am," Harter protested.

"Wait, I get it," I said, peering at the chocolate's surface. "There's his little trunk. In caramel. Wow."

"A little caramel elephant," my mom sighed, "On a chocolate truffle. It's so cute, I hate to eat it." Her voice veered into guilt trip territory.

"Please," Harter insisted. "I make them for people to eat."

"Delicious," my mom murmured over her half, not holding out very long.

"You did *not* buy this chocolate at the Cheese Wheel," I proclaimed, after biting into mine.

"No way," Harter grinned. His smile was like Petry's too, only with spaces where a couple of teeth were missing.

Then I looked over at Petry's smile, where the teeth clung together so cozily, and my brain slipped back into *South Pacific*.

(*Some enchanted evening, someone may be laughing, you may hear him laughing, across a crowded room.*)

And he was.

And I did.

IXL.

In the end (well, at about five in the morning), the hospital let both Petry and me go with instructions to take it easy and see our regular doctors soon. In Petry's case, they also advised him to see his dentist and an ophthalmologist (which was an eye doctor, my mom said), and in my case, since I would be on crutches for a couple of weeks, an orthopedist.

When I finally got up on Saturday, I didn't go out. Sunday was quiet too. I kept checking my email for something from Petry. (His screen name, he'd said, was Stratocaster1, just like the guitars.)

But there was nothing. (Oh, there was plenty of mail from Brad, but I didn't open any of it. I was not in a mood to send someone Pre-Cal homework.)

The only people to even call me were Maddy—"talk about freaking out mom," she chortled—and Deanna, who was both mortified and ecstatic.

I tried to tell myself that maybe Petry's parents were making him rest. Or that he simply had to rest. Or that he'd spent all day at the dentist.

But I couldn't actually believe any of that.

What I believed was that maybe he had only kissed me because he was concussed; that maybe, when he'd woken up, he'd remembered that I had a Hank in the middle of my face.

Or maybe it wasn't Hank—after all, he had said he liked Hank—maybe he'd just realized how uncool I was. (I mean, the guy was a musician. And *not* the Broadway musical kind.)

So maybe now he was too embarrassed to call me. Too embarrassed even to text.

On Monday, I missed school because I needed to get my ankle checked.

On Tuesday, I wended my way in.

I was pretty desperate to see Petry by that time.

I had thought a lot about how soft his lips had been, and (okay, this is silly) about how our noses had just kind of automatically made space for each other. I had thought about that word of his too—resonance.

Nasal resonance. Vocal resonance. Our resonance.

Couldn't we at least be friends?

He wasn't by the school door. He wasn't even at the entrance of the attendance office.

Deanna greeted me with such a big hug she nearly knocked me off my crutches.

A lot of other kids hugged me too. News had gotten around.

Then I ran into Brad.

I realized suddenly that he must have had the Pre-Cal test the day before, Monday. I had totally missed it.

Relief flooded my chest. How could Brad blame me for not helping him cheat if I wasn't even there?

Not that I would have helped him even if I'd been there.

(Seriously, Celia. You would totally *not* have helped him!)

Still, when he left his girl moat to come talk to me, I felt worried. What was I going to say? 'Sorry, I didn't answer your emails.' 'Sorry about the Pre-Cal homework.' 'Um, about that test....'

"You won't be on those crutches long, will you?" Brad asked. "'Cause your story would just be great on the reality show—the girl who saved Eric Clapton's guitar. The TV people will love it."

Did that mean I'd get a part now, even without helping Brad cheat?

I told Brad that my ankle should heal pretty fast. Then tried to feel happy.

But it was hard. Because I realized that I suddenly no longer cared that much about getting a part in the musical. Not if Brad was running the show. And not, well, not with Petry still out. Not calling me. Or texting.

That night, Maddy came down on the train from college to make-sure I was really okay. While we were eating dinner, Deanna's dad, Mr. Zenia, called. He talked to my mom first, who kept saying, thank you, thank you, thank you. Then she handed the phone to me so that I could say, thank you, thank you, thank you. Because the reason he had called was, first, to apologize for Marcel attacking me, and second, to offer me and Petry a reward.

"$5000 a piece," I announced after hanging up.

"He probably wants a release too! In case you guys sue or some-thing. What a cheapskate," Maddy groaned.

"Maddy," my mom protested, "Your sister broke into his shop!"

"I don't think he's a cheapskate," I said. "I think he's terrific."

"And now you're going to go blow it on a nose job." Maddy said.

I was about to say, 'yes!' I was about to shout, 'goodbye Hank!'

Instead, I took a slow deep breath. "As a matter of fact, I'm not."

"You're not?" Maddy exclaimed.

"You're not?" my mom echoed.

"No."

"So, what are you going to do with it?"

"Well," I started. The idea of a guitar beckoned. And guitar lessons. And voice lessons. And college. Always college. Maybe earplugs for my mom—

Then I had another idea.

"You think if I got the pizza guys a new boom box—not a super expensive one, but one that's good enough to have an adjustable bass—you think they'd keep it turned low? The bass, I mean."

"Oh sweetie—" my mom started.

"And maybe we should get a little soundproofing put in my room too," I interjected. "In case I get a mike and an amp or, you know, join a band and have them come over to rehearse."

My mother stopped mid-"pie".

"Right on!" Maddy crowed.

The other news that night was less exciting, though, I confess, it had a certain sweetness.

Pinkwstripes: the reality show's been canceled. You know, the musical.

Bluesong: what do you mean?

Pinkwstripes: the TV people pulled out.

Bluesong: for real?

Pinkwstripes: yeah. Principal Eggars called my dad to see if he could work something out with them after Brad's dad gave up.

Bluesong: seriously?

Pinkwstripes: but they'd already made up their mind. They want somewhere warmer, especially since the school won't let them film inside much, except rehearsals. What they really want is behind the scenes stuff, like what goes on in the girls' bathrooms—

Bluesong: eeuww.

Pinkwstripes: but also, they got way down on Brad.

Bluesong: Brad?

Pinkwstripes: first, he wanted to cast himself for everything, then be director and choreographer too.

Bluesong: he knows how to dance?

Pinkwstripes: he thinks so. And then—this is secret, k?—he went to their office for a meeting and someone saw him ripping off some equipment. Something totally dumb like a stapler, but they got completely p.o.ed—

An orange light came flashing on my screen. It was Brad himself.

For a change, I did not feel giddy; I did not feel panicked; I did not even feel mad. What I felt was kind of sorry for him.

It was not because he was no longer in charge of the musical, it was because, well, the guy seemed to have real problems.

Boymeetsgirl17: yo ceel. I was wonderin' huh?

Bluesong: Brad, about the homework—

I just couldn't give it to him anymore. It wasn't even good for him.

Boymeetsgirl17: Nah, it's not that. Do u do that petition stuff? U know, like your sister?

Bluesong: Huh?

Boymeetsgirl17: the TV people r jerking us around.

Bluesong: you want people to sign a petition about them?

Boymeetsgirl17: yeah, say they're unfair to student labor or something.

Now another orange light came flashing.

Stratocaster1: hey.

My heart skipped, leapt, tap-danced. My heart felt like a combo of Fred Astaire and Ginger Rodgers, Gene Kelly and Debbie Reynolds—a skipping, leaping, tap-dancing, fast-beating—

Okay, so, he'd probably just be my friend, someone I'd been through a lot with, but—

I typed out a couple of quick 'g2g's to Brad and Deeana, then told myself to play it super cool.

Bluesong: hey.

Stratocaster1: how are you?

Bluesong: okay. You?

Stratocaster1: missing you. So much. Sorry i didn't write. They wanted me to rest my eyes, not to look at any screens. I was going to get Harter to text you, then felt too embarrassed.

So, it wasn't because he was embarrassed! I mean, it *was* because he was embarrassed! And concussed!

Bluesong: But you're better now?

Stratocaster1: Just missing you.

Playing it cool suddenly didn't seem such a priority.

Bluesong: miss you too.

Stratocaster1: so you want to get together tomorrow?

Bluesong: sure.

Stratocaster1: great. xxo.

Bluesong: great. xxo.

I signed off. I couldn't take any more messages just then, any more flashing orange lights. As the screen turned blank, my heart filled with song. I didn't know the exact words to it yet, but my heart sang it out anyway, loud and clear.

Celia Pratchett's Partial Compendium of Broadway Musicals (Or Stuff You Might Like To Know About Some Of The Songs In My Head)

Both Deanna and Petry (who are great friends now, btw) have told me that not everyone knows everything about every single great Broadway musical that has ever been written.

I told them that I totally do not know everything about every single great Broadway musical ever written. I have to admit, however, that I probably know more about Broadway musicals than the average person, especially if that average person did not listen to them non-stop as a little kid.

So I have included here some background information about the songs that went through my head during this whole drama.

If you don't know these songs, I highly recommend that you give them a listen.

If you *do* know the songs, I still recommend that you give them a listen. Only in that case, sing along!

1. *The Sound of Music*, i.e. "The hills are alive..." is the title song of (you got it!) *The Sound of Music*. It, like the other songs in *The Sound of Music*, was composed by Richard Rodgers with words by Oscar Hammerstein II. Rodgers and Hammerstein were two of the all time great musical song writers, writing hits like *Oklahoma!*, *South Pacific*, *The King and I*, and about a zillion others.

The Sound of Music was first performed on Broadway in 1959 with Mary Martin and Theodore Bickel. The totally great movie, with Julie Andrews and Christopher Plummer, came out in 1965. The musical is based on the memoir of Maria von Trapp called *The Story of the Trapp Family Singers*.

The Sound of Music is actually a pretty wild story for a musical. A lot of earlier musicals—like the ones with Fred Astaire and Gene Kelley—involved actors who were supposed to be in show business. They were, in other words, actors playing actors. That way, they could justify constantly bursting out in song and dance numbers. *The Sound of Music* was part of a group of musicals that changed all of that. Sure, the Von Trapps had special little "home entertainment" pieces squeezed into the story line, but the musical also features singing nuns, Nazis, and telegram boys.

2.   *People* was composed by Jules Styne, lyrics by Bob Merrill, for the musical *Funny Girl*, which opened on Broadway in 1964, starring Barbra Streisand. The song is not really a standard Broadway musical song—it's kind of pop—and it wasn't actually part of the show until one night during the play's try-outs when Barbra sang it on stage and brought down the house.)

3.   *Till There Was You* is the main romantic song from *The Music Man*, whose music, lyrics and book were written by Meredith Wilson. The musical became a hit on Broadway in 1957; the movie (also great) was made in 1962. The movie features Robert Preston as the conman Harold Hill, and Shirley Jones, as Maaaaarion, Madame Librarian. The early Beatles (!) did a great cover of *Till There Was You*, with Paul McCartney singing the vocals.

4.   Cream has nothing to do with Broadway musicals. It was an awesome British blues/rock band, starring bass-vocalist, Jack Bruce, drummer Ginger Baker, and guitarist-vocalist Eric Clapton. Petry knows a lot more about them than I do, but one of their biggest hits was *Sunshine of Your Love.*

5.   *Sunrise, Sunset* is from *Fiddler On The Roof.* It's a totally heartbreaking musical about a Jewish father dealing with awful times (Tsarist Russia around 1905). Although there are many funny songs, much of the music has a wistful, autumnal quality. One especially nice thing about *Fiddler* is that it has a lot of good women's parts (all those daughters.) The music was written by Jerry Bock, lyrics by Sheldon

Harnick, and book by Joseph Stein. The musical first came out in 1964, movie in 1971.

6. *Before the Parade Passes By* is from *Hello Dolly!* It's also got kind of a wistful quality. Maybe because Dolly Levi, the star, feels like she's getting old. This makes for a great female role as it allows for both crooning and belting. The music and lyrics of *Hello Dolly!* were written by Jerry Herman, the book (for the play) by Michael Stewart. It was based on two of playwright Thorton Wilder's plays—*The Merchant of Yonkers*, from the 1930s, which Wilder then revised into *The Matchmaker* in 1955. Supposedly, Wilder's plays were themselves taken from earlier works—a German play written in the 1840's which was based on an English play from the 1830s. (That's another thing I like about musicals: writers take stories from everywhere, give them great tunes, and make them totally new.)

7. *All I Want Is A Room Somewhere* is from *My Fair Lady*, which is one of my favorite musicals of all time—the music, the dancing, the costumes, the cockney accents, the posh accents—it's all completely brill! The only problem with *My Fair Lady* is that there's only one good female role. In the movie, she was Audrey Hepburn (who not only had a sublimely perfect nose, but a sublimely perfect everything.)

The book and lyrics for *My Fair Lady* were written by Alan Jay Lerner, the music by Frederick Loewe. They are both based on the play *Pygmalion*, by George Bernard Shaw. Shaw's play, in turn, was based on the Greek myth of Pygmalion, the sculptor who fell in love with one of sculptures that then came to life. That Greek myth was also retold by Ovid, a Roman writer. (Crazy!)

The musical was first a hit in 1956 with Rex Harrison and my very very favorite Julie Andrews. The movie, directed by George Kukor, came out in 1964, with Rex Harrison and, as mentioned above, Audrey Hepburn. (The songs in the movie were sung by Marni Nixon.)

Now, I love Audrey Hepburn—she was a great actress and a really kind person—but I object to casting her in the movie in place of Julie

Andrews. Not only was that an insult to imperfectly-nosed singers, but Hepburn, playing the lowly flower girl at the beginning of the movie is so beautiful that it's impossible to imagine her as anything remotely like 'a squashed cabbage leaf.'

8. *Do Re Mi* is from *The Sound of Music* (see above) where Julie Andrews finally got to shine on film as well as on stage.

9. *The Jet Song* ("When you're a jet, you're a jet all the way") is from the amazing *West Side Story*, music by Leonard Bernstein, lyrics by Stephen Sondheim, choreography by Jerome Robbins. It is based on Shakespeare's *Romeo and Juliet*, but takes in New York City in the fifties in the middle of a gang war between the Jets (white working-class) and the Sharks (Puerto Rican immigrants.) The show opened on Broadway in 1957. It is incredibly sad.

10. *I Feel Pretty* is also from *West Side Story*, and it's a lilting, bright, gathered-skirt kind of song. Maria (the Juliet character) sings it in front of some mirrors in a dress shop.

11. "Bed, bed, I couldn't get to bed" is the first line of *I Could Have Danced All Night* from *My Fair Lady*. Eliza sings it in her nightgown, exhilarated after successfully learning how to say *The Rain In Spain Stays Mainly On the Plain*. I used to sing it (to Maddy's great disgust) dancing all over our living room couch.

12. *Who Will Buy?* is one of the greatest songs of many great songs from *Oliver!* (music and lyrics by Lionel Bart, based on *Oliver Twist* by Charles Dickens.) A lot of the song is performed by these vendors who stroll into this fancy London square and then magically start singing and dancing in perfect sync. Don't you love musicals!?

13. *A Spoonful of Sugar* is from *Mary Poppins*, sung in the movie (1964) by the incomparable Julie Andrews who plays Mary Poppins, a kind of magical nanny. The music was written by the Sherman Brothers, it was made by Disney, based on the British *Mary Poppins* novels written by Mary Travers.

14. People don't always think of *The Wizard of Oz* as a movie musical, but it's got tons of songs, and how can you beat the young Judy Garland? She's so sweet and moon-eyed, you just can't help loving her. *Over the Rainbow* was written by Harold Arlen (music) and E.Y. Harburg (lyrics). The movie was made by MGM in 1939, and was based on the book by Frank Baum.

15. *Consider Yourself* is from *Oliver!* sung by the character known as the Artful Dodger.

16. *I'd Do Anything* is also from *Oliver!* It's kind of a Dr. Jeckyll/Mr. Hyde song—half of it, sung by Oliver and Nancy, is super sweet. The other half, sung by Fagin and the Artful Dodger, is less so.

17. *Some Enchanted Evening* is from *South Pacific,* whose music and lyrics were by Richard Rodgers (music) and Oscar Hammerstein II (lyrics), play by Joshua Logan. It takes place in the South Pacific in World War II and was a very brave musical politically, because a big part of its plot focuses on interracial relationships, which were not so well accepted in 1949. (Maddy likes *South Pacific.*) The story was taken from James Michener's *Tales of the South Pacific.*

18. *I'm gonna wash that man right out of my hair!* is also from *South Pacific.* That's another song Maddy likes because she feels it expresses women's independence. But it's also important, she says, that the shampoo *not* be tested on animals. (I agree.)

Acknowledgements

I want first to thank Jonathan Segal for his absolutely wonderful illustrations. Not only do they enliven the book, they energized my personal re-writing process, giving me the faith to finish the project. I want also to thank Amos Segal for his support of this side of the work.

Great great thanks to Heron Haas and Jeannie Hutchins, two terrific editors and friends, for their creativity, wit and attention; their patient help, which extended from plotting to punctuation, was invaluable.

I want also to acknowledge my immeasurable debt to my parents for, among other things, arranging childhood tap dancing and voice lessons; to my brother, Robert, for putting up with all the childhood tap dancing and singing; and finally, to Christina Martin, Meredith Martin, and Jay Martin, for not suppressing the ongoing tap dancing and singing, for their supportive writing commentary, and, most importantly, for being the loves of my life.

K.G.

KARIN GUSTAFSON divides her time between practicing law and practicing writing. She has previously published *1 Mississippi*, a children's counting and bedtime book, *Going on Somewhere,* a book of poetry, and a blog (with elephants) that can be found at http:ManicDDaily.wordpress.com.

JONATHAN SEGAL, a recent graduate of SUNY-Binghamton, has been a lifelong comic and creator of comics. *Nose Dive* is his first illustrated book. (Hopefully, says Karin, there will be many more.)